Six years after completing her training,
Staff Nurse Sarah Williams finds herself
back on the wards. She's the new nurse—
for the second time around—but this time
there's the added complication of her
widowhood, her two children and hostile
Dr John Simmonds!

LOVE'S CURE

BY

MARGARET BARKER

MILLS & BOON LIMITED
15–16 BROOK'S MEWS
LONDON W1A 1DR

First published in Great Britain 1985
by Mills & Boon Limited

© Margaret Barker 1985

Australian copyright 1985
Philippine copyright 1985

ISBN 0 263 75266 6

Set in 10 on 11 pt Linotron Times
03–1285–56,000

Photoset by Rowland Phototypesetting Limited
Bury St Edmunds, Suffolk
Made and printed in Great Britain by
Richard Clay (The Chaucer Press) Limited
Bungay, Suffolk

CHAPTER ONE

SARAH swished the curtains round Mrs Greenwood's bed, and smiled at her patient with a confidence she didn't feel.

'This won't take long, Mrs Greenwood,' she said briskly, as she put the shaving tray at the side of the bed.

'I've been in hospital so many times, Staff Nurse, I don't know why I feel so nervous.'

You and me both, thought Sarah. 'Perfectly under-standable, Mrs Greenwood.'

'Oh, call me May, dear; I'm not that ancient, although to hear these doctors talk you'd think I'd got one foot in the grave. Too old at forty-four indeed! My mother was forty-seven when she had her tenth.'

'And how old was she when she died?' asked Sarah, calmly pulling back the counterpane.

'Oh, I don't know . . . fifty something, I think.'

'Exactly,' said Sarah quietly. 'You've got six healthy children at home who need you, and after your last repair operation, your body is simply not strong enough.' She was glad she'd glanced at the case history. That was one thing she'd remembered from six years ago; always treat the patient as a whole. Even a simple task like a pubic shave required some knowledge of the background.

Her hand trembled slightly as she picked up the razor. Sister Dawson had been right to assign her to junior work on her first morning; it seemed a lifetime since she was on the wards.

'Now just relax, May,' she said, as she spread the dressing towel across her patient. 'Good; nice and still. Is that warm enough?'

'Just right, Staff. I can see you've done this a time or two.'

Oh, thank you for those kind words, thought Sarah, concentrating all her attention on what had once been a routine task.

'There you are,' she said, straightening her back and looking at the anxious, careworn face. 'That was quite painless, wasn't it?'

'Couldn't 'ave done better myself, Nurse,' said May Greenwood, and they both laughed.

Sarah moved the tray and plumped up May's pillows.

'Ooh, what a pretty ring!' said May, catching hold of Sarah's hand. 'You married, then?'

'Yes,' said Sarah, carefully removing her hand.

'Well, that's all right, then, 'cos I've been too scared to ask anybody about my op. I mean, what are they going to do to me?'

The trusting eyes fixed themselves on Sarah, and once again she was glad she knew something about the patient.

'Hasn't the doctor seen you yet?' she asked.

'Well, yes, but you know me . . . struck dumb with embarrassment, I was . . . couldn't understand a word he said, and didn't dare ask any questions. You see, Nurse, what I want to know is . . .'

May launched into a long, confused account of all her medical worries. Sarah sat on the edge of the bed, listening patiently, and answering questions. For a woman who had borne six children, and undergone several operations, May seemed to know surprisingly little about her own anatomy and physiology.

'So you see, May, there's really nothing to worry about,' she said, standing up and straightening the counterpane. Sister Dawson disapproved of nurses sitting on beds, but Sarah had always found it encouraged patients to voice their fears instead of brooding over them. 'You're only six weeks pregnant, so the termination will be relatively simple.'

'Bless you, Nurse! I wish you'd been around when that high-and-mighty doctor was trying to explain . . .'

Her voice trailed off, as her eyes settled on a point somewhere behind Sarah's head.

'I hope you're not referring to me, Mrs Greenwood,' said a deep masculine voice.

May's face creased into a mischievous smile. 'Good Lord no, Dr Simmonds! I was talking about that little man in the pin-stripes—you know, the one with the posh voice.'

'I think you mean Mr Shaw, don't you?' said the voice, and Sarah swung round to look at the barely concealed grin on the face of the Senior Registrar. Dr Simmonds' amusement lasted for a brief second, before the rugged features became serious. 'If you've finished your cosy little chat, Staff Nurse, perhaps we could get on with some work.'

The dark blue, expressive eyes looking down on her were cold and impersonal, with a hint of sadness. His thick brown hair was going prematurely grey at the temples.

'Sister said I might find you here,' he continued in a cool, sardonic voice, 'although she expressed surprise that you were taking so long.'

She would, the old battleaxe, thought Sarah; hasn't changed a bit since I was a first-year on her ward!

'Sister's busy with the other firm, so she would like you to take me round—that is if you can spare the time,' he added sarcastically.

'Yes, Doctor, I'm quite finished here.' Sarah smiled at May before pulling back the curtains and gathering up her tray. 'I'll be with you in a moment, when I've taken this to the sluice.' She might be new on the ward, but she wasn't going to be trampled all over on her first day. Start as you mean to go on, she told herself, as she emptied the water down the sink.

John Simmonds was still standing by the side of May's bed when she returned. He appeared to be having a pleasant chat, but his face clouded over as Sarah approached.

'Come on, Staff, we haven't got all day,' he said brusquely, as he bore off down the ward.

Sarah hurried after him, trying to keep up with his long strides, without actually running. A nurse never runs except in cases of fire, flood . . .

'Pull the curtains, Nurse,' he barked, as they reached a bed at the end of the ward.

The young girl lying on top of the counterpane looked up with a defiant air.

She looks a tough customer, thought Sarah, as she whisked the curtains round. Out of the corner of her eye she could see Sister gesticulating at her from the other side of the ward, where she was efficiently taking Mr Thwaite and his team round their patients. Sister was pointing to her notes trolley. Ye gods! thought Sarah. I've forgotten to bring Mr Shaw's notes, and I haven't a clue about this patient—she's only just arrived.

Sarah hovered in the gap at the end of the curtains. Should she abandon Dr Simmonds yet again while she chased off after the notes?

'Where the devil is that houseman? He's never here when I want him!'

Better not! Sarah closed the gap and moved inside.

The girl eyed them warily. She was chewing bubble-gum, in a loud insolent manner, perfectly aware that she was annoying the tall, distinguished-looking doctor. It won't be long before he loses his cool, she thought gleefully. Just like them useless teachers used to do at school—start hollering and shouting. That would be fun! She smiled to herself as she blew a large bubble. When it gave a loud bang, she waited for the desired effect, but she was disappointed.

'Would you like me to throw that away for you?' Sarah asked quietly, reaching for a tissue.

''Tain't finished yet.'

'Want to save it for later, do you?' asked Dr Simmonds solemnly.

The girl scowled, then slowly and deliberately removed the gum from her mouth, rolled it into a neat ball and stuck it to the side of her water jug.

That'll please Sister, thought Sarah, as she moved towards the reluctant patient.

'It's not my fault,' said the girl ominously. 'I was raped.'

'Yes, so we understand,' said Dr Simmonds, in a soothing voice. He turned towards Sarah. 'Have you got the notes, Staff Nurse?'

'Well, no . . . actually I was just going to get them when . . .'

There was a rustling of curtains and a knight in shining white coat entered, pushing the notes trolley.

'Dr Walker—how nice of you to drop in,' said the Registrar to his houseman. 'And I see you've brought the notes. Staff Nurse will be pleased. She didn't know I would need notes on my ward round. Probably thinks I'm a walking computer.'

No, I think you're an insufferable male chauvinistic pig, but you can't scare me, thought Sarah. What a charming houseman! Like a breath of fresh air . . . I haven't seen him before.

The young doctor shot her a sympathetic glance, while the Registrar rifled through the patient's notes. Sarah looked at the young girl. Under that brash exterior she was clearly very frightened.

'Why don't you lie back on your pillows for a few minutes?' suggested Sarah kindly. 'Doctor just wants to ask you a few questions.'

'I ain't taking my clothes off!'

'Not if you don't want to,' said Dr Simmonds

smoothly. 'But we can't operate tomorrow unless you do. We'll come back later if you prefer . . .'

'I was raped.' Again the same stark, undiluted statement.

Poor girl, thought Sarah. She's going to need a lot of sympathy. 'Come along, Samantha,' she said kindly, after glancing briefly at the notes. 'It is Samantha, isn't it?'

'Sam,' was the sulky reply.

'All right, Sam, let me help you.' Sarah was already turning back the covers, smiling confidently at her patient.

Samantha paused for an instant to look at Sarah, decided she could trust her, and submitted to the examination.

As the two doctors went out, Samantha put out her hand and caught hold of Sarah.

'Will you be here tomorrow, Nurse, when I go down?'

'Yes, I will, Sam.'

'Good.'

It was a simple, basic acknowledgement that she had got through to the girl. Sarah patted her hand.

'I'll be here all day if you need me, Sam.'

It was kind of Sister Dawson to give her an evening off on her first day. At least she could get back home in reasonable time to pick up the children. I wonder how they're getting on, she thought.

'Staff Nurse, could we go on to the next patient, please?'

Sarah shot a sympathetic glance at Samantha and hurried away to the waiting Registrar and his houseman. They were already installed at the next bedside.

'How do you feel now, Mrs Dewhurst?' asked Dr Simmonds.

'Much better, Doctor. That blood you gave me seems to have done the trick.'

Sarah looked at the thin face on the pillow. Several

pints of blood had been necessary to bring her to an operable condition, but she still looked weak.

'Am I going down tomorrow, Doctor?'

'Yes; it's a week since your last transfusion. We'll operate tomorrow,' said Dr Simmonds.

'Thank goodness for that! I feel so helpless just lying here, and my Sid at home looking after the kids all on his own. His sister comes in during the day, 'cos I mean 'e can't take time off or 'e'd lose 'is job. I've lost mine—I was an evening cleaner . . .'

Mrs Dewhurst poured out her troubles, and Dr Simmonds listened patiently, as if he had all the time in the world. When she paused for a few seconds, he turned to Sarah.

'Will you see that the Social Department pay a visit here, Staff?'

'Of course, Dr Simmonds.'

John Simmonds was skimming through the notes. 'Good—all the routine tests were carried out on admission.' He raised his head and looked at the patient. 'Don't worry, Mrs Dewhurst, we'll get your problems sorted out. Now, have you any more questions?'

'No, thanks, Doctor.' Mrs Dewhurst smiled at the tall Registrar, thinking what a handsome face he had.

Sarah was also watching John Simmonds, amazed at his patient bedside manner. He was a good doctor, there was no doubt about that. So why did he have to be so short-tempered with his staff? Perhaps his wife nagged him—Sarah had noticed the broad gold band on his finger. Yes, that was it; his wife didn't understand him, so he took it out on the nurses.

'I'm writing you up for a sedative so that you'll get a good night's sleep tonight.'

'Thank you, Doctor.'

Sarah pulled back the curtains and they moved on down the ward. Sister Dawson came hurrying over from the Thwaite firm for a few seconds. The starched cap was securely anchored on her crimpy grey curls above her beaming face.

'Everything all right, Dr Simmonds?' she asked anxiously.

'Yes, thank you, Sister.'

'I'm sorry I had to leave you with Staff Nurse Williams, especially as she's only just joined us.'

'That's quite all right, Sister . . .'

'Well, you will join us for coffee when you've finished, won't you?' She breezed off, without waiting for a reply.

For the first time, the irascible Registrar seemed to notice Sarah as a human being. He paused at the foot of an empty bed, and the piercing blue eyes swept over her.

'So you're new here?'

'Second time around, you might say,' she replied defensively. 'I trained here, but I've been away for six years.'

'Doing what?' he asked bluntly, but his expressive eyes regarded her with interest.

'I married.'

'I see.' The interest had vanished.

'And had children.' Why did she feel as if she were making a confession? It was none of his business, anyway.

'Poor little mites,' he muttered.

Sarah gasped. 'Why do you say that?' she asked, barely able to conceal her annoyance.

'Because they've got a working mum. Don't you think you should be at home looking after them?'

'They're in school at this precise moment,' she retorted hotly.

'And afterwards?'

'I've made perfectly adequate arrangements,' she replied, moving on to the next patient. Really! It was like the Spanish Inquisition. He was beginning to sound exactly like her mother. The woman's place is in the home . . . well, that's where she'd love to be, if only . . .

Sarah forced herself not to think about Mark. It was tragic, but life must go on.

'This is Mrs Brown, Doctor,' she said in her most professional voice, as she handed him the notes.

'Hello, Mrs Brown. How are you today?' The smooth bedside manner had returned, as John Simmonds fixed his attention on his patient.

Dr Walker smiled sympathetically at Sarah, and she returned his look gratefully.

As Sarah was preparing Mrs Brown for examination, Mr Shaw himself arrived. Alan Walker held back the curtains deferentially so that the consultant could enter. He was followed closely by Dr Smith, the anaesthetist.

'Good morning, Dr Simmonds,' said the great man. 'Where's Sister?'

'She's with Mr Thwaite, sir,' replied the Registrar. 'She's doing a round with him.'

'No, she's not,' snapped Mr Shaw. 'There's no one out there at all except a couple of juniors.'

'I'll see if I can find her, sir,' said Sarah hurriedly.

'Who are you?' the consultant asked abruptly.

'Staff Nurse Williams, sir.'

'And how long have you been with us?'

'I—er—I started this morning . . .'

'Well, that's no good, is it? Go and get Sister, there's a good girl.' The consultant shook his head in exasperation, and out of the corner of her eye Sarah noted the smug expression on the Registrar's face. She felt like an incompetent first-year. Silently she went out and hurried down the ward.

As she thought, Angela Dawson was holding court in the side-ward, simpering girlishly as she poured coffee for her beloved Mr Thwaite. Probably the highlight of her day, thought Sarah uncharitably.

'Mr Shaw is on the ward, Sister,' she said quietly.

A harassed look crossed the plain, broad features.

'Well, can't you take him round, Staff Nurse?'

'He's asking for you, Sister.'

'Oh, very well, Nurse.' She gave Sarah a withering look. 'Can't think why I gave Staff Nurse Fielding that long weekend. I'm too soft with my nurses, Vincent,' she added, her tone softening, as she smiled at Mr Thwaite. She was always absolutely correct with the medical staff on the ward, but enjoyed being familiar in the privacy of her own side-ward. Sarah's assumption was correct; her coffee sessions were the highlight of her day. At forty-eight, she was beginning to think life had passed her by. She was good at her job, having done nothing else for the whole of her adult life. But it would have been nice to get into administration, or even to get married, and have children . . .

And here was young Nurse Williams—Nurse Gibson as she was before she married that poor Dr Williams. She'd had everything, and yet here she was back on the ward where she started. Angela Dawson smiled suddenly at Sarah.

'Take over from me here, Staff Nurse. Two lumps for Mr Thwaite, if you please,' she added, before she swept out of the door.

Sarah stifled a grin. Take over from me, indeed! Anyone would think she was performing a major operation!

Mr Thwaite relaxed visibly when Sister had gone. He looked up at the new staff nurse, thinking that her face looked familiar.

'Aren't you going to have a cup with us, Staff?' he asked kindly. Sarah hesitated, wondering what Sister's reaction would be. 'Staff Nurse Fielding usually joins us,' he added helpfully.

'Well, in that case . . .' Sarah poured herself some coffee and sank down into one of Sister's shabby but comfortable armchairs. It was the first time she'd relaxed since early morning, when she'd got the children ready for school.

'Tired, Nurse?'

The question was a friendly one, but Sarah was quick to assure Mr Thwaite that she was fine.

'Haven't I seen you somewhere before?' he asked.

'Probably,' she replied. 'I was on this ward six years ago—before my son was born.'

'Of course—now I remember,' said the consultant. 'You worked right up to the last minute, as I recall . . . I thought I might have to deliver you one morning, when you had backache.'

Sarah laughed. 'I remember thinking the same thing myself. But we needed the money, so I kept working as long as I could.'

'So it was a boy, you say?'

'Yes. He's called David,' Sarah said proudly. 'And then I had Fiona a year later.'

'Didn't waste much time, did you?'

'No; we'd set our hearts on a large family . . .' Sarah's voice trailed away, as the all too familiar ache came back.

'I was sorry to hear about Mark,' said Mr Thwaite quickly. 'You're a brave girl, coming back to work so soon afterwards.'

'It's three years since.' Sarah's voice sounded dull and lifeless.

'As long as that? Well, you take care of yourself, my dear, and if there's anything I can do to help, you've only to ask. Young Mark was a great favourite of mine. He was an excellent doctor.'

'Thank you, sir.' Sarah took a large gulp of coffee.

'Look, Nurse, I want to dash off before Sister arrives back, or I shall be here all day,' he said with a wry grin. 'Give her my apologies, will you?'

'Of course, sir. I've got to get back on the ward myself.'

She walked to the door with him, and he held it open with a delightful show of old-fashioned courtesy. What a friendly man he was—especially for a consultant. She remembered that Mark had always liked him.

'Thank you for the coffee, Nurse Williams.'

'It was a pleasure, sir,' she said, with feeling. It was so nice to have a link with the past—with the days when she was young and carefree and so much in love.

Sarah spent the rest of the morning helping the new admissions to settle in. She was ready for a break at lunchtime. Going down the corridor to the staff dining-room, she was pleased to hear a familiar voice.

'Sarah! So you've actually made it!'

'Liza!' Sarah exclaimed with delight, as a tall blonde Sister caught up with her.

'You said you wanted to come back, but I never thought you'd do it, Sarah,' said her friend. 'So what happened to the parental opposition?'

'Oh, it's still there, but I'm ignoring it. Dad's OK, but Mum thinks I'm mad.'

'Well, I think you're very wise, Sarah. Are you on your way to lunch?'

'Yes, I'm absolutely starving; been up since the crack of dawn, Liz.'

The two friends chatted excitedly as they went into the dining-room.

'You haven't changed a bit since we were in PTS, Sarah,' Liz was saying. 'After all you've been through . . . Who's looking after David and Fiona?' she asked, hastily changing the subject when she saw the pain in Sarah's liquid brown eyes.

'They're in school during the day, and Joanna Lindley takes care of them when I'm not there. She's stuck at home all day, so it's a nice little job for her. I think she enjoys the extra cash—in fact it was her idea in the first place.'

'I haven't seen Joanna since she got married. How is she?'

'Fine. She's got a dear little boy, Christopher. He's two and a half.'

'Well, well; all my friends having children,' said Liz. 'I'm beginning to feel like an old maid!'

Sarah looked enviously at Liz's expensive hairstyle, tucked away under the smart Sister's cap.

'It's not easy being a mother,' she said quietly.

'No, I don't expect it is,' Liz agreed quickly. 'Well, tell me about your first morning on the wards.'

Sarah recounted the exploits of the dreaded Sister Dawson, and they both had a good laugh. When she came to describe her meeting with Dr Simmonds, Liz interrupted her.

'Oh, he's really quite nice when you get to know him, Sarah. He hasn't been here long, so I think he's just shy.'

'Rubbish! That's not shyness. I think he's got a nagging wife,' retorted Sarah.

Liz laughed. 'Well, if he has, he keeps her well hidden. Nobody's ever seen her.'

'Perhaps he keeps her chained up at home, then. He said that's where I ought to be,' added Sarah.

'He didn't!'

'Yes, he did, Liz. I couldn't believe anyone could be so rude.'

'He's always been terribly correct with me—haven't seen much of him, though. Well, I mean, there's not much call for a gynaecologist on male orthopaedic, now, is there?'

They both laughed.

'So what are you doing over here at the Women's, Liz?' Sarah asked.

'Visiting my aunt; she's having a D. and C. on Cavell,' replied Liz. 'I was off duty this morning.'

'The food hasn't changed,' remarked Sarah, as she swallowed another mouthful of shepherd's pie.

'Eat it up, Nurse,' said Liz, imitating the broad Scots accent of their Sister Tutor from PTS days, and suddenly the years seemed to roll away, and nothing had changed.

If only you could do that . . . put the clock back and start again, thought Sarah wistfully. She returned quickly to the present, and finished her lunch. Got to keep your strength up when you're a working mum.

'Must dash, Sarah,' said Liz, standing up. 'I'm on duty in five minutes.'

'Me too,' Sarah said. ''Bye, Liz.'

''Bye, Sarah.'

They both went their separate ways, but Liz paused for a moment to watch her friend go off down the corridor. Poor girl, she thought—imagine being widowed at twenty-five! And they were so much in love. They simply lived for each other. She remembered the day Mark died—it seemed like yesterday, but it must be three years ago now.

Yes, that's right, because I was staffing on Male Medical, and they brought Mark in suffering from cerebral haemorrhage. He was only twenty-eight—he'd been on duty all day, and there he was, lying pale and still on the trolley.

Liz shivered and strode off in the other direction. She remembered going off duty that evening. That was the last time she saw Mark. He never recovered consciousness.

CHAPTER TWO

SARAH pushed open the swing doors and went back into Nightingale Ward.

'Thank goodness—another pair of hands!' said the small plump staff nurse. 'I'm Pam Fielding. You must be Sarah Williams—Sister told me you'd be back soon. She's off duty this afternoon.' Sarah gave an audible sigh of relief, and Pam laughed. 'Bad as that, was she?'

'I think she gets worse,' said Sarah. 'She still thinks I'm a first-year.'

'Yes, you've worked for her before, haven't you? I remember you were a staff nurse when I was still in PTS. It must seem very strange coming back after so long.'

'It does . . . well, what would you like me to do?' Sarah asked briskly.

'Medicines, please. Take Nurse Crabtree round with you. She needs the experience—prelim exams next week.'

Sarah found the medicine trolley and set off round the ward with Nurse Crabtree. The medicines hadn't changed much, but there seemed more of them. She had barely finished when the ward doors swung open and the visitors started to arrive, in a flurry of flowers and Lucozade.

The questions flowed thick and fast—When is she going down to Theatre? What time is the op? Can we visit in the afternoon? How long will she be in?

Sarah and Pam were kept fully occupied, trying to set everyone's mind at rest. Halfway through the afternoon, as things began to ease off, Pam beckoned to Sarah.

'Come and have a cuppa, while it's quiet,' she whispered.

Thankfully Sarah followed her into the side-ward and sank down into the nearest chair. She eased off her flat-heeled brogues and twiddled her black-stockinged feet.

'That's better!' she sighed.

Pam switched on the electric kettle, and smiled sympathetically at Sarah. 'The first day is always the worst,' she said.

'Yes, I'll soon get used to it, I'm sure,' Sarah agreed.

Pam made the tea, and chatted on about hospital social life and gossip, the forthcoming dance in the Nurses' Home, her latest boy-friend . . . It all seemed light years away from Sarah's own little domestic world out at Riversdale. She suddenly felt much older than her twenty-eight years.

'We've got to finish the consent forms before Sister gets back,' said Pam, when they had finished their tea. 'Samantha Brown's going to be a difficult one. We've got to get her mother's signature. She was just arriving when we came in here.'

'I'll get it if you like,' Sarah volunteered.

'Have you seen her mother?'

'Well, no,' Sarah replied uneasily, wondering what she'd let herself in for.

Pam grinned. 'Rather you than me! Here's the form. Off you go—and the best of luck!'

Sarah went back into the ward and made for Samantha's bed. If the mother was anything like the daughter, it was not going to be easy. She stopped at the end of the bed and surveyed the large lady who was perched precariously on a small stool, scowling at Samantha.

'Mrs Brown?' Sarah began tentatively.

'What do you want?' The large lady extended the scowl to include Sarah, as well as her daughter.

'I'd like you to sign a consent form for your daughter's operation,' replied Sarah firmly.

'There's no need to tell the whole ward!' snapped Mrs Brown, looking anxiously round at the other visitors. No one was the least bit interested in Mrs Brown or her daughter, but she continued her hostile staring at Sarah. 'Bring it here, Nurse. I'll sign anything, so long as we can get this over and done with.'

Sarah was about to hand over the form when Samantha spoke up for the first time.

'Draw them curtains, Mum. We don't want everybody watching us.'

'Draw them yourself, you lazy . . .'

Sarah hastily pulled the curtains round; some of the visitors were beginning to take an interest. She sat down on the edge of the bed.

'You do realise what you're signing, Mrs Brown? I mean, has everything been explained to you?' Sarah asked gently.

'Course it 'as. Look, give me that form and let's get on with it.'

Sarah handed Mrs Brown the form and a Biro, then watched as she scribbled her name.

'There you are, Nurse.' Mrs Brown had actually stopped frowning, but the angry look returned as she looked at her daughter. 'Of all the ungrateful girls! After all I've done for you . . .'

'I've told you what 'appened, Mum!' shouted Samantha.

'Keep your voice down, stupid! You've told me— there's no need to tell the 'ole bleedin' 'ospital!'

'Oh, go away, Mum,' cried Samantha, large tears beginning to roll down her cheeks. 'You never did understand.'

In reply, Mrs Brown lifted her right arm and gave her daughter a resounding slap across the face.

'You're not too old for me to put you over my knee!' cried the irate mother.

'Mrs Brown, please,' put in Sarah hurriedly, 'I think it

would be better if you were to leave Samantha now . . .'

'Don't worry, Nurse—I'm off, especially if she's going to turn on the waterworks.' The large lady heaved herself off the stool and glared ominously at her daughter. 'You be'ave yerself,' was her parting shot, as she walked out through the curtains, straight into a tall, white-coated figure.

'Ooh, beg yer pardon, Doctor. You come to see my Samantha, 'ave you?'

'As a matter of fact . . .'

'In a right state she is, Doctor. Don't know what they've been doing to 'er,' said Mrs Brown, beating a hasty retreat.

'Staff Nurse, what is going on here?'

Sarah turned to face the Senior Registrar. His eyes were flashing angrily, as he surveyed the sobbing patient and the distraught staff nurse.

'Everything under control, sir,' said Sarah, with a calmness she didn't feel. It was no good upsetting the patient further. 'Samantha . . .'

'Sam,' corrected the young girl, in between her sobs.

'Sam had a difference of opinion with her mother, that's all,' Sarah explained patiently.

'She slapped me round the face!'

'You poor girl.' Dr Simmonds' voice had a soothing effect. He reached out his long, tapering fingers and smoothed back the fiery red hair from Samantha's swollen face. 'Let's have a look, shall we? Mm, good thing you're not going out tonight, Sam.'

The sobbing ceased, as quickly as it had started. The young girl smiled up at the doctor, thinking he was quite dishy for his age—must be at least thirty.

'Couldn't you have prevented this—er—this little altercation, Staff Nurse?' the doctor asked quietly.

Angrily Sarah raised her eyes to his, and he noticed, for the first time, how expressive her eyes were when she was roused, while she thought what a pompous idiot he was to make such a fatuous remark.

'She couldn't 'ave done nothing, Doctor,' put in Samantha. 'When my mum gets cross, there's no 'olding 'er!'

Sarah suppressed a smile. 'If you don't need me, Dr Simmonds, I'll be getting on with my work,' she said.

'Don't go!' pleaded Samantha.

'Nurse has work to do,' said Dr Simmonds gently.

'But I want to ask her something.'

'Yes, Sam?' said Sarah.

The young girl stared at Sarah, then at the Registrar, before lowering her gaze. 'Oh, forget it,' she mumbled. 'You probably wouldn't understand, anyway.'

'Well, if you remember what it was you wanted to ask, Nurse will be only too pleased to help, won't you, Nurse Williams?' said Dr Simmonds.

'Of course,' replied Sarah. 'Would you like me to leave the curtains closed for a while, Sam?'

'No, pull 'em back. I like to see what's going on.' The girl was her old aggressive self again.

Dr Simmonds caught up with Sarah when she was halfway down the ward.

'I'd like to examine the new Wertheim's as soon as possible, Staff. Would you give me a buzz when her relatives have gone?'

How considerate of him, thought Sarah. He doesn't just barge in and send the visitors away.

'They've been here a long time, Dr Simmonds. I think they're about to leave,' she said helpfully.

'Oh, well, in that case, perhaps you could give me a hand.'

Sarah led the way across the ward. Mrs Davis was saying goodbye to her husband and daughter.

'Can you spare me a minute, Doctor?' asked Mr Davis. 'It's about my wife's operation . . .'

It took several minutes to answer all the questions.

Pam sidled up, and Sarah whispered that she would stay with Mrs Davis while Dr Simmonds examined her.

'Shall I get the inspection trolley?' asked Pam, with a smile.

'Oh, yes, please,' replied Sarah gratefully, wondering how long it was going to take her to get back into hospital routine.

The examination went without a hitch, Patricia Davis was a cool-headed, calm individual, who understood the seriousness of her condition and had accepted that radical surgery was necessary.

'Thank you, Nurse,' she said, with a brave smile, as Sarah made her comfortable at the end.

Her quiet fortitude made it easier for Sarah to forget her experience with Mrs Brown. This was what nursing was all about. Some you win, some you lose.

'Have we had a blood group and crossmatching yet, Staff Nurse?' asked Dr Simmonds, replacing his stethoscope round his neck.

'No; I'll phone Pathology,' replied Sarah.

'Good girl!'

She looked up in surprise. Was he being patronising? The cool, bland expression in those deep blue, searching eyes gave nothing away. Hurriedly Sarah stacked the trolley and made for the treatment room, where she stayed until she was sure John Simmonds would be clear of the ward. She busied herself packing drums for the steriliser. When she emerged, the last of the visitors were disappearing.

'These are my big sons, Nurse,' called May Greenwood, in a cheery voice, and the two teenagers coloured in embarrassment as they made for the door.

'Mind how you go!' shouted May. 'And tell your father to come tomorrow.'

'OK, Mum.' The boys waved hastily, and vanished through the door.

'They're good lads,' said May proudly. 'Their father's

told them I'm having me tonsils took out, but I don't think they believe him.' She gave a quick laugh. 'You've got to look on the bright side, I always say. What're you in for, dear?' This last remark was addressed to a frightened-looking young woman who had arrived during visiting.

May will be good for her, thought Sarah. We ought to have a few more like her on the ward.

Sister came back on duty at five, and made a beeline for Sarah.

'Well, how've you got on, Nurse Williams?' she asked abruptly.

'Fine, thank you, Sister,' replied Sarah.

'Coming back again tomorrow, then?' Sister smiled at her own little joke.

'If you'll have me,' quipped Sarah.

Sister pursed her lips. 'Make sure you have a good night's sleep, Nurse. It's theatre day tomorrow.'

Sarah went out to the front of the Hospital for Women, affectionately referred to as the Women's, and made her way to the staff car park. Her small red car was waiting for her, and she climbed thankfully in and started the engine. It had taken all her savings to buy it secondhand, but it was her first step towards independence. If she could save something from her nursing salary, she would be able to buy a small place for herself and the children, and they could move out of her parents' home. It was a pity she'd given up the flat in Bradfield, but she had been so unhappy after Mark's death that everything her mother suggested had seemed like a good idea at the time.

She drove round the corner, past the Bradfield General Infirmary, which was the main hospital, from which the Women's was an annexe. The nursing staff and doctors moved freely between the two. In front of the Town Hall, the traffic was jammed solid, and Sarah sat in the midst of it, tapping her fingers on the wheel and worrying about the children. Not that there's anything to worry about, she told herself firmly. Joanna is a trained nurse, like me, she can cope with any emergency, but still it would be nice to be there with them.

The traffic started to move, and Sarah breathed a sigh of relief as she let in the clutch. A car pulled alongside and, glancing idly at the driver, she gave a start of recognition; the long, tapering fingers on the wheel, the dark hair, with a hint of grey at the temples. John Simmonds nodded briefly towards her before shooting ahead.

Sarah watched the dark blue Mercedes until it was out of sight. Home to his mystery wife, she thought, as she turned off into the Riversdale road.

The traffic eased off as she left Bradfield behind. As the green fields came into sight, she wound down the window to get a breath of fresh air. Mm, that's better! she thought. The grimy walls of the town had given way to picturesque limestone. Soft, undulating hills rose away from the industrial plain. Sarah automatically reduced her speed, as the pretty, unspoilt village of Riversdale came into view. The pace of life was different here. She drove slowly down the main street of the village and stopped in front of a tiny cottage. The front door led straight out on to the street, so this was rarely used during the day, because of the children. Sarah parked the car and made her way through a covered alley between Joanna's cottage and the next one.

The back garden was awash with toys, but the children were inside the cottage. Sarah secured the childproof gate before tapping on the door.

'It's only me, Joanna.'

'Come in, Sarah . . . the door's not locked. I'm just giving them their tea,' called Joanna.

'Mummy, Mummy!'

Two little bodies hurled themselves at Sarah, and two pairs of sticky hands reached upwards. She sank into the nearest chair and pulled the children on to her lap.

'My, how I've missed you!' she smiled, as she held them to her.

'I've painted you a picture, Mummy . . . want to see it?' asked David.

'Of course. Hello, Joanna, everything OK?' Sarah asked as David went off to find his picture.

'Fine,' replied Joanna, pushing aside the teatime debris and carrying little Christopher across to join the welcome party. 'We've had a lovely time since we fetched David and Fiona from school, haven't we, Christopher?'

'Car,' said Christopher eagerly.

'Oh, yes—David's been playing with Christopher's car. I think Chris wishes he had an older brother. Cup of tea, Sarah?'

'Mm, lovely!'

'Here's my picture, Mummy!'

'Why, that's beautiful, David!'

'It's Grandma feeding the hens.'

'Yes, I thought it was; I recognised her blue pinny. And that's Grandpa, isn't it?'

'How did you know, Mummy?'

'Because he's smoking his pipe.'

'Car, car!' shouted Christopher.

'Would you like to play in the garden with the car again, David?' asked Joanna hopefully. 'You're so good with Chris.'

'All right, if you want me to,' David replied importantly.

'I want to stay here and talk to Mummy.' Fiona's small voice was almost lost in the general hubbub, as the boys dashed out into the garden. 'I'm glad you're home, Mummy.'

'And I'm glad I'm home, darling,' said Sarah, cradling the little five-year-old soothingly in her arms.

'Did you have a good day, Sarah?' asked Joanna.

'So-so,' was her noncommittal reply.

Joanna laughed. 'What does that mean?'

'It means I feel terribly rusty.'

'Well, of course you do—six years is a long time, but you'll soon get back into the swing of things,' said Joanna reassuringly.

'Theatre day tomorrow . . . honestly, Jo, I'm scared!'

'Oh, you'll be fine. It'll all come back to you. I wish I were going in tomorrow.'

'Do you, Jo?'

'Yes, I do,' replied her friend firmly. 'I really miss hospital life.'

'But you've got Brian and Christopher and your own home . . . and everything,' Sarah finished lamely.

'That's right, you remind her how lucky she is,' said Joanna's husband, pushing the door open.

'Brian darling!' Joanna jumped to her feet and kissed him.

Sarah looked the other way. How wonderful it would be to have my husband home at the end of the day, she thought sadly.

'Got to dash,' she said quickly. 'Come along, Fiona, Grandma will be wondering where we've got to.'

Brian put a pile of exercise-books on the table.

'More marking?' asked Joanna.

''fraid so . . . a schoolmaster's lot is not a happy one.' He sat down at the table, moving the plates to one side.

'Thanks, Joanna.' Sarah moved towards the door. 'My mother's going to take them to school in the morning, so if you can collect them afterwards . . . ?'

'No problem—look forward to it. You're on duty till eight, aren't you? Brian will take them home at bedtime, while I'm bathing Chris.'

'Come along, David; leave that car . . . 'bye, everybody!' called Sarah.

Sarah piled the children in the back seat, complete

with all their belongings, then started the engine. As they cruised along the main street, several people waved to them. There goes that poor young widow with the two children. Plucky little thing . . . I hear she's gone back to nursing . . . best thing to do . . . keep her mind off it . . .

There was a light on in the kitchen as Sarah pulled into the farmyard. In the gathering dusk she could see her mother toiling over a large mound of dough at the kitchen table.

'I'm all behind today,' said her mother, without looking up from her task.

'Hello, Grandma, I've done a picture of you!' announced David.

'Just put it down there, love, till I get my hands out of this flour, there's a good boy.'

Sarah looked at Joan Gibson's thin grey hair, tied back in a severe knot at the back of her head. She looked much older than her fifty-six years, and here she was adding to her problems.

'Would you like a cup of tea, Mum?' she asked gently.

'No, thanks—I haven't time. I've got to get this bread in,' was the weary reply.

'Well, I'll take the children upstairs, then.'

'Yes . . . the water's hot. Good night, my darlings; give Grandma a kiss . . . that's nice.' She raised her head for a moment and returned to her work.

Sarah took the children upstairs and got them ready for bed. She spent longer than usual over their bedtime story, and her own eyes were beginning to droop along with Fiona's as she finished.

'Now you will be good tomorrow night, when Grandma puts you to bed, won't you?' she said, as she tucked them in.

'Of course we will,' replied David sleepily.

'Grandpa's going to read you a story,' Sarah added.

'Oh, goody! I like Grandpa's stories. 'Night, Mum.'

'Good night. Sleep tight.'

Sarah tiptoed out, pausing at the door to take a final look at the two fair heads on the pillows. David was beginning to look so much like Mark. She put the light out and went downstairs into the big, warm kitchen, filled with the delicious smell of baking bread.

'Here she comes,' said her father, puffing contentedly on his pipe by the fireside. 'What sort of a day did you have?'

'It was very good, Dad.' Her voice sounded confident. 'I enjoyed it.'

He looked pleased.' That's my girl! I knew you'd be all right. I remember the day you started school, I said to Mother . . .'

Sarah smiled to herself as she listened to the familiar story. Her father had always been so proud of her.

'What time are you on duty tomorrow, Sarah?' he asked, at the end of the saga.

'Eight o'clock, Dad.'

'You'll have to be up with the lark, then. I'll give you a shout when I start the milking.'

'Thanks.' Sarah stood up. 'I'm going to have an early night.'

'Aren't you going to stay down for some cocoa?' asked her mother, as she lifted the loaves from the oven.

'No, thanks, Mum. I'm all in.' It slipped out without thinking. She didn't want her mother to know how tired she really was.

Joan Gibson sniffed disapprovingly and pushed a stray lock of grey hair out of her eyes.

'Well, if you will have these silly ideas about returning to work . . .'

'Good night, Mum; good night, Dad.' Sarah escaped quickly up the stairs, not wanting to hear all the arguments again.

She passed Julie's bedroom and peeped in. The room was empty, but the bed was made up, ready for Julie's weekend off. Dear little sister, she thought; I do miss her now she's in PTS. I can't believe she's eighteen! She moved on to her own bedroom.

It was the same little room she had had when she was a child; the same whitewashed walls, pink carpet and bedspread; antique washbasin on the marble washstand. There was a view from the window across the fields to the hills. Sarah had often sat in the window-seat when she was a romantic teenager, wondering who she would marry. And then this wonderful man had come along and swept her off her feet. They were married for four idyllic years. It hadn't mattered that they never had enough money, that Mark had to work long hours as a houseman. What they had had together was something special, unique, a once-in-a-lifetime experience.

Sarah put out the light and closed her eyes. No one could replace Mark . . . she was determined that no one ever would. She had her career and her children—that was all she needed now.

CHAPTER THREE

THE ward was humming with activity when Sarah arrived on duty next morning. The night charge nurse was ready to give her report at Sister's desk.

'Come and join us, Nurse Williams,' Sister Dawson ordered crisply, glancing up at the clock on the wall.

No cause for complaint, thought Sarah thankfully. It was still only two minutes to eight, although it felt like the middle of the morning. She adjusted the small starched white cap on the top of her coiled-up long mid-brown hair. It felt even more precarious than yesterday. I must get it cut as soon as possible, she thought.

'Now, Nurse Williams, if you're quite ready, we'll ask Nurse Hamilton to give us her report.'

For some reason Sister Dawson preferred to take the report standing up, so this meant that her staff swayed around the desk, or clung on to it for support if they were feeling tired. This was the way she had been trained, and she disliked change. Sarah would have liked to take the weight off her legs for a few minutes, after her early morning rush, but she listened intently to the report, anxious to learn as much as possible about her patients.

'. . . Samantha Brown was restless during the night.'

'Wasn't she written up for a pre-op sedative?' snapped Sister.

'Yes, but she refused to take it, Sister,' replied Nurse Hamilton quickly.

'Oh, well, she had only herself to blame, then.'

'She seemed slightly delirious at one point.'

'In what way, Nurse?'

32

'She was talking . . . er . . . all kinds of nonsense, Sister.'

'Nonsense! Did you try to unravel this . . . er . . . nonsense, Nurse?'

'There wasn't time, Sister.'

'Wasn't time! You should have made time, Nurse. I suppose I'll have to have a word with her myself,' said Sister wearily. 'She's a strange girl. I believe she's first on the list—yes, here we are—Nurse Williams, would you do her pre-med as soon as the report is finished, please. She's going down at nine.'

'Yes, Sister.'

As Nurse Hamilton came to the last patient, Sarah went off to the treatment room. Samantha was written up for omnopon and scopolomine; Sarah prepared the hypodermic syringe, placed it in a kidney dish, then gathered together the other requirements—theatre gown, socks, cap, and wrist label.

Samantha Brown, age 16, she wrote on the label. Poor girl—only sixteen, all her life in front of her. Sarah went down the ward with her equipment.

'Good morning, Sam,' she said to the prostrate figure under the covers.

'Go away!' was the muffled reply.

'Wakey-wakey . . . rise and shine! We've got to get moving,' Sarah persisted.

'I've been awake all night, and now you come waking me up, just when I want to go to sleep,' grumbled Samantha sulkily.

'You can go to sleep again when I've finished a few little routine jobs.'

'Can I have a drink?'

'Sorry, Sam; not till you get back from Theatre,' replied Sarah firmly. 'Now, pop along to the loo and spend a penny, there's a good girl.'

The bright red hair on the pillow moved, and a sad-looking face stared up at Sarah.

'God, I feel awful,' she said, in a small, pitiful voice.

Sarah smiled sympathetically, and held out her hand in an encouraging gesture. Samantha took hold of her hand and hauled herself out of bed. She padded off down the ward in her bare feet, before Sarah had time to find her slippers. I hope Sister doesn't see her, she thought, as she pulled the curtains round the bed.

Samantha returned as Sarah was finishing making up the bed as a pre-op. The canvas stretcher sheet was over the mattress and the top sheets turned back. Samantha stared at the waiting theatre gown.

'Put this on, Sam,' said Sarah briskly.

'Do I have to, Nurse?'

'I'm afraid so.' Sarah helped Samantha off with her nightdress. 'And now these socks, please, and the cap . . . Now I'll just fix this round your wrist . . . there we go!'

She turned away to pick up the syringe. Large round eyes watched her apprehensively from beneath the sheet, but Samantha seemed to have given up. She remained perfectly still and quiet, as Sarah gave the injection.

'Now you can go back to sleep, Sam, and when you wake up . . .'

'Nurse!' Samantha's strangled cry was so full of anguish that Sarah recoiled in horror.

'What is it, Sam?' she asked, regaining control of herself.

'I can't go through with it!'

Oh, no, not at this late stage, when everything had been set in motion! 'Why not, love? What's the matter?' Sarah asked gently.

'Because I love him,' was the quiet reply.

'Love who, Samantha?'

'My boy-friend. I wasn't really raped . . . I just made that up 'cos I'm scared of my mum. I don't think she believes me, but she's kept quiet, so's I'd get my operation . . . but I want my baby!'

Samantha started to cry in heartrending sobs. Sarah sat down on the bed, saying quietly,

'Do you want to talk about it?'

The young girl rubbed her eyes and looked up at Sarah. 'He's in the Army—my boy-friend,' she added in a proud voice. 'He's twenty; he asked me to marry him ages ago, but my mum wouldn't let me. His mum's all right—she likes me. I haven't told them I'm pregnant, and he's coming home on leave tomorrow . . . Oh, God, Nurse, what am I going to do? You've got to help me!'

Samantha grabbed hold of Sarah's hand and stared at her beseechingly.

'I'd better have a word with Sister.' Time was ticking on . . . the Theatre was all prepared.

'No! Don't leave me!'

Sarah sat down again; a plan of action was forming in her mind.

'What's your boy-friend's name?' she asked.

'Jim,' Samantha replied lovingly.

'And his mother?'

'Mrs Priestley—she likes me, Nurse. I wish I'd told her instead of my mum . . .'

'Yes, well, is she on the phone, Sam?'

'Yes—I can give you the number—will you ring her, Nurse?'

'We'll see—write it down here, Sam . . . thanks. Now, you just lie back and rest for the moment, and I'll see what I can do.'

Sarah slipped out through the curtains. The pre-med was already taking effect; Samantha's eyes were beginning to droop. She would have to hurry.

'What was all that about?' asked Sister sharply, when Sarah reached her desk.

'Samantha Brown wants to cancel her termination,' she replied breathlessly.

'Oh, come now, Nurse, the child must be delirious! She was raped, you know.'

'No, she wasn't. Let me explain, Sister.'

'You'd better ring Theatre and explain to the surgeon; she's on Dr Simmonds' list.'

Just my luck, thought Sarah, as she hurried to the phone.

'Hello, Theatre Sister here.' The voice at the end of the line was cool and efficient.

'Sister, this is Staff Nurse Williams, Nightingale Ward. We have a young patient, Samantha Brown, first on Dr Simmonds' list for a termination. She's changed her mind.'

'I'll see if I can find Dr Simmonds for you,' was the impersonal reply.

Sarah hung on to the phone as the seconds ticked rapidly away.

'I'm afraid Dr Simmonds has been delayed, Nurse Williams, but I'll give him your message as soon as he arrives.' The line went dead, and Sarah was left staring at the phone. What should she do now?

On impulse she took the hastily scribbled number from her pocket and asked for an outside line.

'Hello.' The woman's voice gave no indication of its identity.

'Mrs Priestley?' asked Sarah hopefully.

'Yes, this is Mrs Priestley.'

'This is Staff Nurse Williams, at the Hospital for Women. We've got a young patient called Samantha Brown in here . . .'

'Oh, yes, she's a friend of Jim's,' put in Mrs Priestley, in a friendly voice.

'She'd like to see you, if that's convenient, Mrs Priestley.'

'Well, what time's visiting, Nurse?'

'It's this afternoon and this evening, but do you think you could come in before then?'

'Well, if little Sam wants to see me, I will. I was just on my way out to the shops, so I'll pop in. She's not in any danger, is she, Nurse? My Jim thinks the world of her . . .'

'No, she's not in danger, Mrs Priestley,' Sarah put in quickly. 'But she'll be pleased to see you. She's on Nightingale Ward.'

'All right, I'll come as soon as I can. Goodbye.'

As Sarah put the phone down, the doors from the corridor burst open and a young theatre porter came through, pushing his trolley importantly in front of him.

'Samantha Brown,' he announced. 'Which bed, Staff?'

'There's been a slight hitch,' Sarah told him hurriedly. 'You'd better take the second on the list.'

The young man frowned. He disliked changes in routine.

'My orders are to collect Samantha Brown,' he said rigidly, as he pushed the trolley into the ward.

'The operation has been cancelled!' Sarah called after him.

He paused and stared at her in disbelief. 'On whose instructions, Staff?'

'We're awaiting a call from Mr Simmonds.'

'Well, that's no good, is it? Sister, what's all this about a cancellation?'

Sister Dawson hurried down the ward, frowning ominously.

'Did you get through to Dr Simmonds, Staff Nurse?' she demanded.

'He's been delayed; they're going to inform him as soon as he arrives.'

'Oh, very well. Take Mrs Greenwood; she's next on the list, and she's had her pre-med. Nurse Crabtree, help this porter with Mrs Greenwood. Here are the notes . . .' Sister flew off again like a harassed mother hen.

Sarah hurried down the ward to take a look at

Samantha. The young girl had fallen into a quiet, untroubled sleep, so she tiptoed out again.

'Pre-med for Mrs Davis, Nurse Williams,' called Sister.

'Yes, Sister.'

'Goodbye, everybody!' May Greenwood was still chirpy, in spit of the pre-med. 'Don't I look glamorous?' she said to the young porter who was pushing her out through the doors. 'What do you think of me socks, eh?'

She stuck a wool-clad foot out from under the red blanket, and the serious young porter grinned, in spite of himself.

'Very nice, missis,' he conceded, as they moved off down the corridor.

Sarah went across the ward to prepare Mrs Davis for her Wertheim's operation. It was going to be a long, complicated operation, but she had been well prepared, and even managed to smile while Sarah was giving her the pre-med injection.

'If I'm not properly round when my husband comes, will you ask him to wait, Nurse?' she asked.

'Yes, of course.' Sarah fixed the wrist strap on. 'That's not too tight, is it?'

'No, that's fine, Nurse. How's that young girl with the red hair? I heard her crying in the night.' Pat Davis's face mirrored her concern.

'She's got problems, but nothing that can't be solved,' replied Sarah, wishing she felt as confident as she sounded. It was typical of Mrs Davis to be concerned for someone else, at the moment when she was facing a major operation herself. She smiled at her patient. 'Is there anything else you need?'

'No, thanks, Nurse. I'm looking forward to having a nice long sleep,' she replied, returning the smile.

Sarah went out into the ward.

'Will you start the medicines, Nurse Williams?'

'Yes, Sister.' She had just reached the medicine trolley when the swing doors of the ward burst open and a tall, irate figure came storming towards her. 'I might have known it would be you!' snapped the Senior Registrar. 'I have to learn from a theatre porter that a new staff nurse has rearranged my list!'

'But I left a message with Theatre Sister.' Sarah stood her ground, as she faced the furious surgeon.

'Well, I never got your message,' he continued angrily. 'So what's it all about?'

'Come into the side-ward, Dr Simmonds,' said Sister, hurrying down the ward. 'You too, Nurse Williams.'

'Now, perhaps you'd like to explain,' the doctor began, in an icy voice, as Sister closed the side-ward door.

'Yes, I'd like to hear the full story, too,' added Sister sternly.

Calmly Sarah recounted the facts.

'But you say you'd already given the pre-med when the patient said she didn't want to go through with it?' Angela Dawson queried.

'Yes, Sister.'

'But doesn't that suggest that it might have been the effects of the drug, Nurse?' she persisted.

'I don't think so, Sister,' replied Sarah firmly. 'The pre-med hadn't had time to take effect when she told me. She's asleep now, of course . . .'

'So we've only got your word for it,' interrupted John Simmonds hotly.

'I'm afraid so, Doctor,' was her quiet, submissive reply.

'Oh, well, you were quite right to cancel the operation, Nurse. We have to be one hundred per cent certain in cases like this. It's a very serious operation, not to be undertaken lightly.'

Sarah found herself fascinated by the expression in his blue eyes. He seemed almost human, as he discussed the grave moral issues at stake. She found herself agreeing with everything he said. He certainly knew his subject.

'Well, I must get back to Theatre, ladies,' he finished off, dazzling them both with an unexpected smile that lit up the distinctive, rugged charm of his face. 'I was held up this morning, and I had a late start.'

He should smile more often, thought Sarah; it makes him look positively handsome. I wonder why he was late . . . perhaps he had a row with his wife . . .

He was making for the door . . . better confess, before he goes, she thought.

'I took the liberty of phoning Mrs Priestley, the boy-friend's mother,' she told him. 'She's coming in this morning.'

'You did what, Nurse Williams?' This from Sister was what Sarah had expected.

'Goodbye, ladies. I'll be along later,' Dr Simmonds said quickly. 'I'll leave you to sort things out.'

Oh, charming! thought Sarah. Talk about leaving the sinking ship! Still, I suppose he's got a busy morning in Theatre.

'I phoned Mrs Priestley, Sister. I think Sam's going to need an ally against her mother.'

'In future, I'd like you to consult me!' snapped Sister.

'Yes, Sister.'

'But as you've taken such an interest in the case, perhaps you'd like to see it to its conclusion. I've got a busy ward to run.' Angela Dawson gave Sarah a long, hard look, and decided that she would make a very good staff nurse once she had settled in and learned to toe the line again. She had always thought she was a promising junior. But it didn't do to let these young nurses know what you were thinking. Keep them on their toes . . .

'Thank you, Sister; yes, I would like to help Samantha all I can.'

'Well, see if you can finish the medicines before Mrs Priestley comes,' Sister said brusquely.

Sarah hurried back to the medicine trolley and made her way carefully round the ward. She was just washing the medicine glasses and spoons at the end of the round, when a small, plump middle-aged lady stepped nervously inside the ward. Sarah, who had been keeping her eye on the door, noticed her at once and hurried down to meet her.

'Mrs Priestley?' she asked.

'Yes, I've come to see Samantha.' The woman looked warily round the ward.

'Would you like to come in here for a moment? There's something I must tell you first.' Sarah led the way into the side-ward. Quietly and calmly, she explained the situation.

'Poor girl,' said Mrs Priestley. 'How she must have suffered! You see, Nurse, I know her mum, and she's a very difficult woman. But I'll stand by her, don't you worry. You did right to ring me. Can I see her now, Nurse?'

'She might be a bit drowsy, Mrs Priestley.'

'That's all right. I'd just like to take a peep at the dear little thing—I've known her since she was a baby. Never had a chance, poor little mite, but I'll look after her now. She should have come and told me in the first place.'

Sarah led the way down the ward and peeped inside the curtains. Samantha seemed to be asleep. As Sarah approached the bed she opened her eyes, then a smile of happiness crossed her face as she saw Mrs Priestley.

'Mam!' she cried, holding out both arms.

The older woman leaned forward and embraced her, and Sarah decided to leave them alone. When she returned a few minutes later, they had sorted the problem out. Mrs Priestley was going to have a word with Samantha's mother, and was going to return tomorrow with her son, when he came home on leave.

'Can she stay another day, Nurse?' asked Mrs

Priestley anxiously. 'I'd like to sort everything out before Jim gets home.'

'Yes, I'm sure that can be arranged,' Sarah told her.

'Thanks, Nurse.' Samantha was looking happier than she had done since she came in. 'Can I see the dishy doctor again? You know, Nurse—old Blue Eyes,' she grinned.

'If you mean Dr Simmonds, I'll see what I can do. Now, say goodbye to Mrs Priestley, Sam.'

'Goodbye, Mam, thanks for coming,' said Samantha.

'Don't worry, love; I'll take care of you . . .'

'And you'll go and see my mum?'

'Yes, of course I will. Goodbye.' Mrs Priestley kissed the anxious face and followed Sarah out. 'I don't mind admitting, Nurse, I'm not looking forward to seeing Mrs Brown. She can be very awkward,' she confided, when they were out of earshot.

Sarah gave her a sympathetic glance, 'Yes, are you sure you can cope?' she asked anxiously.

'Of course I can. Takes more than Flo Brown to scare me!'

'Well, good luck, Mrs Priestley,' smiled Sarah.

'Thanks, Nurse—I'll need it!'

Sarah watched the plucky little woman set off down the corridor. When she returned, Sister was waiting for her.

'Well, Nurse Williams, how did it go?' she asked anxiously.

'She's going to look after Samantha, when she's discussed it with her mother. I said she could stay until tomorrow.'

'Of course. Thank you, Nurse, you've been a great help,' Angela Dawson said quietly. 'Now, if you'd like to get on with the pre-meds—the list is on my desk.'

She hurried away, leaving Sarah with the feeling that she was getting back some of her old confidence.

The morning passed without further hitch. By the

time Sarah went off for lunch, the first cases were back
on the ward. Some were still unconscious, but a few of
the minor ops had had their airways removed, been
washed, and were sitting up and taking notice. She took
a look round the ward before she left, and had a feeling
of satisfaction. It was always good to see the patients in
their own nightdresses after a successful operation, with
a look of relief on their faces. Well, that wasn't so bad
after all, they seemed to be saying.

The staff dining-room was crowded when Sarah arrived for the second sitting at one-thirty. She collected a
plate and helped herself to chicken and boiled potatoes,
before looking around for a table.

'Sarah! Over here,' called a familiar voice.

'If it isn't my little sister!' Sarah made her way across
the crowded room. 'What are you doing here, Julie?' she
asked, in surprise.

'Came to see how the other half live. There's a place
here, Sis.' Julie was busy moving aside some plates.

'Thanks.' Sarah sank down beside her sister and gave
her an appraising look. 'Mm, you look good in uniform.'

'Do you think so?' asked Julie, looking down at her
pink check dress and starched white apron. 'I can't keep
this flour bag on, though!' She put a hand to the cap on
her head.

Sarah laughed. 'You'll have to suffer as we all did in
PTS. It's meant to hold all your hair out of sight.'

'It's meant to make you look as unattractive as
possible!' declared Julie hotly. 'Which in my case isn't
difficult.'

'Oh, Julie,' said Sarah laughingly. She took a close
look at her little sister. The mousy brown hair was
escaping from beneath her cap, the thin face was a little
pale, the tiny nose just a wee bit too pointed . . . but the
eyes! They were lively and expressive and full of fun,
as usual. 'You've got more than your regulation curl
showing, Nurse,' she pronounced, with mock severity.

'I'm glad you think it's a curl. It feels more like a rat's tail—I wish I had your hair, Sarah.'

'Well, you're welcome to it, because I'm thinking of having it cut.'

'You're not!'

'Yes, I am. I haven't time to fiddle around, fixing it up all the time,' Sarah declared firmly, as much to convince herself as anyone else.

'Whatever will Mum say?'

'Mum doesn't have to wear a starched cap all day. Don't look so worried, Julie; I'll get it done properly. I won't just hack it off myself.' Sarah concentrated on the chicken for a few moments. It was tasty and she felt hungry after her long morning. 'So you thought you'd come over and have a look at your big sister, did you?'

'Our two o'clock lecture was cancelled, so I'm free until three-thirty. Are you off duty now, Sarah?'

'I've got a two-five, then I'm on till eight. I thought I'd go shopping; have you got time to come with me, Julie?'

'No, I've got to swot. We've got a test on the digestive system this afternoon.' She pulled a face.

'Don't worry, little one; PTS doesn't go on for ever.'

'It seems like it. Will I see you at the weekend?' Julie stood up and swung her red-lined, full-length black cape round her.

'I don't know yet. Sister hasn't done the off-duty—I hope so.'

'So do I. 'Bye, Sarah.'

Sarah watched the tiny figure negotiating her way through the tables. It seemed incredible that her little sister was old enough for the Preliminary Training School. She still looked as if she should be in the village school. Perhaps it was because she was the baby of the family. Sarah felt a pang of anxiety. Unlike the rest of them, Julie had simply drifted into a medical career, because that was what Dad had thought would be good for her. He had been disappointed because he couldn't afford to take up his scholarship and become a doctor. He was always needed on the farm; that was why he had encouraged his own children towards medicine. Sarah's early success in her nursing exams had made her father very proud. And then Anne, two years younger, had followed in her footsteps and was now a Sister in the QA's; Mike, now twenty-four, had recently qualified as a doctor in London. But dear little Julie, with her head in the clouds . . . Sarah shook her head as she watched her sister disappearing through the dining-room door.

She finished her meal and went off to the changing room, on the ground floor of the Nurses' Home. It seemed such a waste, having three hours off duty now, but it was too far to go home and back again before five o'clock. She changed into her outdoor clothes, thick tweed suit and sweater—there was a definite nip in the air after the long hot summer. It would soon be autumn, and then winter—and the ordeal of Christmas. That was when she most missed Mark.

CHAPTER FOUR

THE main street of Bradfield was crowded with shoppers. As Sarah headed for the large department store, she passed a trendy-looking hairdresser.

I wonder if they could fit me in this afternoon? Probably not, she thought hopefully, as she went inside. Loud pop music was blaring out from hidden speakers in the roof, and there was an unpleasant smell of perming solution. Sarah's resolution died on her and she turned to make her way out again.

'Can I help you?' asked a thin, unsmiling receptionist with pink frizzy hair.

'I . . . er . . . I don't suppose you can fit me in this afternoon, can you?'

'Come this way, please.' It was too late to escape.

Half an hour later, as Sarah walked out into the street, she had to admit that the stylist had made a good job of it. She glanced at herself in a shop-window . . . oh, very chic! Sort of elfin. Her chin seemed more pointed, somehow, and her eyes looked different. It would take some getting used to, but it would certainly be easier to manage. She stepped inside the big department store and took the lift up the restaurant for afternoon tea. Quite like old times . . . tea and cakes in Sandersons during a two-five had been one of her little treats before she was married—only at the beginning of the month, of course!

The cakes on the trolley all looked delicious. Sarah chose a chocolate éclair.

'You're lucky, you don't have to watch your figure,' said the friendly waitress, looking enviously at Sarah's trim waistline.

Sarah smiled up at her, thinking how Mark had always urged her to put on a bit of weight, so she would be strong enough for their large family. She glanced at her watch. The children would be coming out of school, and Joanna would be there to meet them. I wish I could see their little faces, she thought. I'd much rather be at the school gate than sitting here like a lady of leisure. Soon be time to go back on duty.

She finished the éclair and poured herself another cup of tea. This was the time when she most wanted a cigarette. After Mark's death, she had smoked like a chimney, regardless of the fact that it was ruining her health. When she had begun to think clearly again she had forced herself to stop. It hadn't been easy, but she was over the worst now. She would never allow herself to be tempted—she'd seen too many chest patients, coughing their last in hospital, and still begging for a cigarette, in spite of what tobacco had done to them.

The evening rush hour had started when Sarah made her way back to hospital. Schoolchildren dashed past her, swinging their satchels, working wives hurried to get home before their husbands, impatient motorists honked their horns in the inevitable traffic jam, and everywhere there was an air of expectancy, a going-home kind of feeling. An ambulance screeched into the hospital unloading bay, and a stretcher was carried inside.

Sarah went into the Nurses' Home and changed into her dark blue staff nurse's uniform. She looked in the mirror, as she fixed the little starched cap. My, she thought, that was a lot easier! It was a great weight off her mind. She crossed the road and went into hospital.

Sister Dawson looked up from her desk when Sarah arrived on the ward.

'What have you done to your hair, Nurse Williams?' was her blunt greeting.

'Don't you like it, Sister?' Sarah countered.

'It's not a question of whether I like it or not, Nurse. It seems such a waste to have it all cut off like that. You've always had long hair, haven't you?'

Sarah nodded.

'I remember when you first came to me from the PTS . . . still, I suppose it will be easier to manage. Pull up a chair, Nurse.'

Sister Dawson must be feeling tired, thought Sarah, as she sat down to receive the report, and no wonder, when she glanced down the list of post-operative patients.

'Now you're sure you can cope, Nurse Williams?' asked Sister, not unkindly. 'It's early days for you, I know.'

'Don't worry, Sister, I shall be fine.'

'Staff Nurse Fielding will be back from tea in a few minutes, and you've got Nurse Crabtree and Nurse Rothwell . . .'

She continued to fuss around the desk, and Sarah breathed a sigh of relief when she actually went. She could see that the two juniors had already started on the beds and backs, so that left her free to check on the post-ops.

A second-year nurse had been assigned to special Mrs Davis, now back from Theatre after her Wertheim's operation.

'Everything all right, Nurse?' asked Sarah, glancing at the blood pressure and TPR charts.

'Yes, Staff, Mrs Davis is doing remarkably well.'

'I thought she would.' Sarah smiled down at the frail but brave-looking face. 'How are you feeling, Mrs Davis?'

'I'm fine,' she replied, in a hoarse whisper. 'Is my husband here, Nurse?'

'Not yet. I'll send him over when he arrives.' Sarah briefly adjusted the intravenous drip before moving on to the next patient.

Pam Fielding came back from tea, and elected to do

the medicines. It took Sarah a whole hour to get round
the post-ops, and then it was time to serve supper to the
patients who could eat. May Greenwood was insisting
she was hungry.

'I always eat after my operations, Nurse,' she said,
with a grin. 'I could eat a horse!'

'Sorry, no horse tonight, May. How about some nice
savoury mince?'

'Not again!'

'Or an egg custard?'

'Don't be daft, Nurse—that's baby food. Give me
some mince. Beggars can't be choosers. I hope my Bob's
going to bring me something nice tonight.'

Sarah served out May's supper, and Nurse Crabtree
took it across to the bed. As she put her spoon back into
the heated trolley, the doors swung open and Alan
Walker came in. The fair-haired houseman smiled when
he saw Sarah, and walked down the ward to station
himself in front of the trolley.

'Got anything nice in there, Staff? I'm feeling a bit
peckish; been in Theatre all day.'

'Just the usual,' she said. 'Can't you wait for your own
supper?'

'Haven't time to go in this evening . . . I'm going to
meet a few friends in the Black Bull. Why don't you join
us when you come off duty?'

'Sorry—I've got to get home,' was her automatic
reply, but she felt pleased to be asked.

'Well, some other time, perhaps.' He glanced down at
her wedding ring, and made a mental note to find out
about that. 'I came to have a look at today's cases. Any
problems?'

'No, everything's under control. Give me a few minutes to finish the suppers and I'll come round with you.'

'That's OK,' said Nurse Fielding, coming down the
ward from the treatment room. 'I'll take Dr Walker
round.' She gave him a dazzling smile. He was obviously

one of her favourites. Not surprising, thought Sarah;
he's quite a charmer.

She finished serving the suppers just as the visitors
started to arrive, and they kept her busy with certificates
to sign and questions to answer. As soon as she was able,
she made a further round of the post-ops, checking
blood-pressures, blood loss, discharges, pulse rates. Mrs
Dewhurst's intravenous drip had stopped. Sarah tried to
adjust it, but it was no use; the vein appeared to have
collapsed. It would have to be replaced. She looked
around for the houseman.

'He left the ward a few minutes ago,' volunteered
Nurse Crabtree.

Probably in the pub by now, thought Sarah. I could fix
a new IV myself, but I'd better stick to the rules. She
rang the switchboard.

'Nightingale Ward—can you find someone from the
Shaw firm to set up a new IV?'

'OK, Nurse; will do.'

The visitors were beginning to leave. Sarah went
down the ward to have a chat with Samantha, because
she had been all on her own. She was in fine form.

'I'm glad my old lady didn't come, Nurse,' she said
cheerily. 'She'd only have caused trouble.'

That's true, thought Sarah.

'You just wait till you see my Jim tomorrow, Nurse—
he's gorgeous!'

Sarah smiled and moved away. The last visitors were
going out through the door. From somewhere in the
middle of the ward there was a piercing scream.

'Get away from me! I know you're going to kill me!'

A couple of visitors turned back into the ward to see
what was happening.

'Get rid of the visitors!' Sarah ordered the startled
Nurse Rothwell, as she made towards the commotion.

Nurse Crabtree, deathly pale, was backing away from
Mrs Tate's bed. 'I didn't do anything, Staff. I went to

change her water jug, and she screamed at me.'

'That's all right Nurse,' Sarah told the frightened junior, wishing she hadn't sent Staff Nurse Fielding off to early supper. She looked at the ominous, staring eyes of the distraught patient. Her mind searched for details of the case . . . there was no time to look through the notes. She remembered that Jean Tate had been admitted two weeks ago for hysterectomy. There had been post-operative complications, which was why she was still here, but she had always been a quiet, inoffensive little woman, the sort of patient you barely noticed was there.

'Don't come any nearer!' Jean Tate shouted, as Sarah made a move. 'I know you're all plotting against me!'

Persecution mania, diagnosed Sarah. She had seen it once before in a patient. It had come on very quickly; the patient had the delusion that everyone was against her.

There was a loud crash as Mrs Tate smashed a bottle against the side of her locker.

'Go and ring Security, Nurse Crabtree,' whispered Sarah.

'Stay where you are!' called Mrs Tate, in a menacing voice. She was holding the broken bottle above her head, and looked as if she was about to throw it.

The terrified patients were frozen into silence. Something had to be done to break the deadlock.

'Now come along, Mrs Tate,' said Sarah quietly, inching her way towards the bed. 'I'm not going to hurt you. Why don't you let me help you? If you just put the bottle . . .'

'No!' It was a long piercing cry from the heart. 'I don't want to live any more!'

The deranged patient had hauled herself out of bed and thrown wide the window. As Sarah took another step forward, she turned to face her, still holding the broken bottle.

'Let me die,' she said quietly. Her eyes still fixed on Sarah, she started to climb out of the window.

There was the noise of the ward door opening. It distracted the poor patient for an instant, and Sarah saw her chance. She knocked the broken bottle from Mrs Tate's hand and threw both arms round her. The woman struggled with the superhuman strength of the insane, and Sarah felt herself losing the battle, even as she saw the long drop outside the hospital window below her.

Suddenly she felt herself being pulled back inside. Strong, firm arms were holding her safe, while she still held on to the struggling patient.

As he relaxed his grip on her, the Senior Registrar turned his attention to Mrs Tate.

'Just a little something to help you sleep,' he was saying soothingly, as he swiftly injected the patient.

Mrs Tate became very still and quiet, and Sarah cast a grateful look at Dr Simmonds.

'Thank you very much, sir,' she said quietly.

'That's all right, Nurse. I thought you were coping admirably when I came in, but another pair of hands is always useful in cases like this.' His expressive blue eyes seemed to pierce inside her.

She rubbed the place where his strong arms had held her and shivered unexpectedly. He noticed at once.

'I expect you're suffering from shock, Nurse,' he said gently.

'No, I'm all right,' she replied, then, suddenly re-membering, 'Mrs Dewhurst needs a new IV. I thought Dr Walker would be coming,' she finished lamely.

'I'll change it when Mrs Tate is asleep,' he said, then in a gentler tone, 'How are you feeling now, Mrs Tate?'

There was no answer from the slumbering form.

'Would you ring Psychiatric, Nurse Williams, and get someone here as soon as possible. She'll have to be transferred, tonight. She should respond to treatment. And when you've rung Psychiatric, go and make yourself a cup of coffee. Here's Nurse Fielding; she can take over here.'

A startled Pam Fielding was coming down the ward, listening to the garbled accounts from the patients, who had all started to talk at once.

'It looks like I've missed something,' she said to Sarah.

'Certainly have—Dr Simmonds will fill you in. I've got to ring Psychiatric.'

When she had made the phone call, Sarah slipped into the side-ward, put the kettle on, and sank into a chair, gently easing off her shoes. Mustn't be too long.

She had drunk her coffee and was about to go back into the ward when the door opened, and startled, she looked up to see the tall figure of Dr Simmonds.

'I was just coming, Doctor,' she said, trying desperately to fit her feet back into their shoes. For some unknown reason they seemed to have swollen.

'That's OK, Nurse. Nurse Fielding can cope out there. You've earned a rest. Besides, I was hoping you might make me a cup of coffee. I've got to wait till the psychiatric firm arrive.'

He lowered himself into one of the armchairs, stretching out his long legs in front of him. Sarah busied herself with the coffee jar. She could feel his eyes on her. She still hadn't succeeded in putting on her shoes, and she knew he was looking at her black-stockinged feet.

'Thank you, Nurse Williams,' he said, as he accepted the cup from her.

To hide her embarrassment, Sarah made herself another cup and sat down again. There was an awkward silence before he asked,

'Doesn't your husband mind you working in the evenings?'

Sarah swallowed hard. 'I'm a widow,' she replied quietly.

'Oh, I'm sorry; I had no idea.' She looks too young to

be even married, let alone widowed, he thought. And children too . . . very sad.

'I've come to terms with the situation, now,' she continued, quietly, then paused. Why on earth am I confiding in him? she thought. He's the last person I should be talking to like this . . .

He reached across and put his arm on the back of her chair. His fingers rested lightly against her starched uniform, and a quiver of excitement ran through her body. Somehow the nearness of that virile, masculine frame began to unnerve her. She turned her head and saw that his liquid blue eyes were looking enquiringly into hers with an earnest expression that belied comprehension. Holding her breath, she waited in anticipation, but his eyes clouded over.

'In some ways it makes it easier . . . not having a partner, I mean,' he said in a matter-of-fact kind of voice.

What a callous thing to say! thought Sarah.

'Especially in the medical profession, where we have to work long hours.' He had caught her startled look. 'I know what I'm talking about,' he continued.

I doubt it! Sarah wanted to tell him.

'My wife is no longer with me, and I wouldn't go through all that again,' he said coldly.

I bet they had a terrible divorce, and she stung him for every penny . . .

'Yes, well, I certainly will never get married again, but for quite different reasons from you,' said Sarah, finally succeeding in wiggling her toes inside her shoes. 'Now, if you'll excuse me, I must go and see how Nurse Fielding's getting on.'

There was a prickling sensation behind her eyes as she hurried back on to the ward. That man had the most uncanny way of upsetting her. She made a vow to herself to avoid him at all costs in future, except in professional situations.

Sarah stayed on for a further half hour after the night staff arrived, because there was so much to be done. When she finally reached the car park, she had to will herself to stay awake at the wheel. At least the traffic was lighter at this time of night.

The lights of Riversdale came into sight, sparkling like a cluster of diamonds in the darkness of the valley. She switched off the engine and let herself in the house.

Her father was in his favourite place by the fireside, puffing away at his pipe. Winter and summer alike, he always had a fire in the grate in the evenings. His wrinkled, weatherbeaten face lit up when she came in.

'Hello there, lass. Have you had a good day?'

'Yes, thanks, Dad. How are the children?'

'Good as gold,' he said proudly. 'I read them a story—or two,' he added, smiling. 'I couldn't get away.'

'You'll have to be firm with them, Dad.'

'Nay, lass, they're only young once. I remember when you were their age . . .'

Here we go again, thought Sarah, sinking down by the fire.

'. . . so you see, children never change, do they?'

'No, Dad. I'll go up and take a look at them, and then I'm going to bed.'

'Good girl; your mother's asleep already. She's been a bit tired lately. Well, good night, then. Same time tomorrow?'

'Yes, please, Dad.'

David stirred and murmured something in his sleep, when Sarah looked in to give the children a kiss, but Fiona didn't move at all. She tiptoed out again. It was almost too much trouble to get undressed. As she lay in the small narrow bed, all alone and decidedly chilly, she thought about the enigmatic Dr Simmonds. What could he possibly know about marriage? Wouldn't go through that again, indeed! I'm sure his wife would agree with him, she thought.

She tried to put their conversation out of her mind, but somehow his face kept coming back to her, just when she was trying to drift off to sleep.

CHAPTER FIVE

SARAH removed her cuffs, rolled up her sleeves, fixed on her frilly working cuffs and made for the treatment room. Her first task next morning was to re-insert Mrs Davis's catheter.

'I'm sorry to be such a trouble, Nurse,' apologised Patricia Davis, when Sarah arrived at the bedside. 'I didn't know it had slipped out until Sister had a look.'

'That's perfectly all right,' Sarah said, swishing round the curtains. 'Now, if you could turn on to your back, like this . . . good . . . let's see . . .'

Sarah prepared her patient and inserted a sterile catheter before making her comfortable again.

'Thanks, Nurse, that's much better.'

Sarah checked the dressing; there was some discharge from the drainage tube. 'I'll be along later to clean that up. Are you comfy now, Mrs Davis?'

The patient smiled her reply. 'How's the poor woman who got so upset last night?' she enquired.

'She's in the psychiatric ward. They've got a very good team. She'll get the best treatment,' Sarah replied.

'You were very brave, Nurse . . .'

'All in a day's work, Mrs Davis.'

The ward doors swung open, and the Shaw firm arrived. They're early, thought Sarah, as she went to Sister's aid.

'Nurse Williams, the trolley!' Sister called, hurriedly rolling down her sleeves as she went to meet Mr Shaw and his staff.

'The new staff nurse can take us round, Sister,' said Mr Shaw unexpectedly. 'What's your name?'

'Nurse Williams, sir.'

'Well, Nurse Williams, my Registrar tells me you were something of a heroine last night . . . Did you know that, Sister?'

'Oh, you mean the psychiatric patient.' Sister frowned. It didn't do to praise the nursing staff. After all, she was only doing her duty.

'Precisely,' Mr Shaw replied, in his clipped, refined voice. 'So I'd like to see if Nurse Williams has what it takes to make a good nursing Sister. She could be useful to us in the future.'

Sister Dawson looked puzzled. I hope he doesn't think I'm near retiring age, she thought . . . not at forty-eight! She made a mental note that she would have her hair done—perhaps she'd find out where Sarah Williams had been for hers.

'I'll be in my office if you need me, Nurse Williams,' said Sister, nodding distantly at Mr Shaw. He's never liked me, she thought, and the feeling is definitely mutual! Not like Vincent Thwaite—now, there's a gentleman—always was, even when he was in medical school.

Sarah started to pull off her working cuffs.

'Oh, don't bother with all that protocol, Nurse Williams,' snapped Mr Shaw. 'Let's get on with the round. Besides, you've got very pretty arms, hasn't she, gentlemen?'

Dr Simmonds looked as embarrassed as Sarah felt, but Alan Walker agreed heartily with his chief.

'Quite a suntan you have, Nurse,' continued the consultant relentlessly as they walked down the ward, followed by the admiring entourage. 'I presume you went on some exotic holiday.'

'No, sir; I live on a farm,' she replied quietly, mortified by the chief's unwanted attentions.

'Do you, indeed?' he said in surprise, suddenly at a loss for words. When he resumed, he was his usual exacting self. 'The notes, Nurse!' he barked.

Sarah was kept on her toes for the next half hour, answering questions, producing the correct notes, explaining dressings, diets, charts, sorting out medication . . . She breathed a sigh of relief as Mr Shaw went out of the door. He was followed closely by his houseman, but the Registrar paused for a moment and turned back into the ward. Sarah looked up at him questioningly.

'You'll be pleased to know, Nurse Williams, that the psychiatric firm think Mrs Tate's condition is merely temporary,' he said, fixing his blue, piercing eyes on her face.

'I thought so myself, Dr Simmonds; I've seen persecution mania in a patient once before, and that also culminated in a suicide bid.'

The friendly eyes became hostile again. 'Who said anything about persecution mania, Nurse?' he snapped.

'Well, that's what it seemed like, Dr Simmonds.'

'Thing are not always as they seem, Nurse. You would do well to remember that.'

'Yes, but . . .'

'I have to go now.' He turned and went out of the door, leaving Sarah annoyed with herself for having let her guard down. The less she said to Dr Simmonds the better.

She started the list of dressings, finishing off with the swabbings.

'Ready for coffee?' asked Pam Fielding, as Sarah unloaded her trolley in the treatment room.

'You bet!' Sarah put the last kidney dish in the steriliser and followed Pam to the side-ward.

Sister emerged, wreathed in smiles as she ushered Mr Thwaite into the ward. 'Only five minutes, Nurses,' she whispered as they passed, her charm vanishing momentarily.

'Yes, Sister.'

'Only five minutes!' fumed Pam, as she poured out the

coffee. 'She treats us like juniors. What about all the extra time we put in when we should be off duty?'

'Drink your coffee, Pam. You'll never change Angela Dawson—she's one of the old school.'

'Do I smell coffee?' Alan Walker's fair head appeared round the side-ward door.

'Come in,' smiled Pam, jumping to her feet to fetch another cup.

'I thought you did very well with the old man this morning, Nurse Williams,' the young houseman remarked, sitting down beside Sarah.

'Which old man is that?' asked Sarah dryly.

Alan Walker grinned. 'Mr Shaw, of course. You surely didn't think I meant John Simmonds? He's not that old—probably about thirty-five, I should say.'

'Just likes to behave like the older generation to keep us all on our toes.' A touch of bitterness had crept into Sarah's voice.

'My, my, he has upset you, hasn't he?' Pam handed Alan his coffee.

'No, he hasn't,' retorted Sarah. 'I just wish he wouldn't behave like a consultant, when he's still only a registrar.'

'He's getting into practice,' said Alan. 'Rumour has it that when Mr Thwaite retires . . .'

'Oh, no!' groaned Sarah.

'You really dislike him, don't you?' Alan looked puzzled.

'I think he's unbearable . . . I'm going back in the ward, Pam. Our five minutes is up.' Sarah got to her feet.

'Creep!' said Pam. 'I'll be along in a minute.'

'Don't hurry.' Sarah sensed that Pam was dying to get Alan Walker on his own.

She was right about this, and Pam was annoyed that Alan wanted to talk about Sarah, when she had gone. She didn't like the interest he was taking in Sarah, especially when he heard she was a widow.

It was time to serve the patients' lunch. Sister was still busy with Mr Thwaite, so Sarah enlisted the juniors to help her with the light diets for the abdominals and low-residue for the vaginal hysterectomies.

'I'll take over now, Nurse Williams.' Sister flashed a charming smile at the retreating figure of Mr Thwaite. 'Would you like to go to first lunch? It might be a good idea, as you're in charge this afternoon, and there's the Samantha Brown case to sort out. I'll brief you on that when you get back.'

'Yes, Sister.' Sarah made for the door. She hadn't had time to talk to Samantha this morning, but the young girl seemed happy enough.

She had a quick lunch in the dining-room, and returned to find Sister champing at the bit.

'I know you're early, Nurse Williams, but I've made a hair appointment, and I'd like to get off duty.' Angela Dawson had decided to play safe, and rung up her own hairdresser. Better the devil you know . . . 'I've made a list of the relatives I'd like you to see . . . and if you're in any doubt about Samantha, you must get hold of Dr Simmonds. She will of course be seen in Outpatients soon, so that we can make the necessary obstetric arrangements.'

When Sister had gone, Sarah went down the ward to see Samantha. She was fully clothed in an attractive green woollen skirt and sweater, that set off the golden-red colour of her hair as she sat on the edge of her bed, carefully making up her face.

'Not too much, Sam. Your skin looks fine as it is.' Sarah smiled down at her patient.

'Oh, hello, Nurse. Do you think I should wear my false eyelashes?'

'No, I don't,' laughed Sarah. 'You're not going in for a beauty competition, you know!'

'Yes, but Jim's coming,' said Samantha happily. 'I can't wait to see him.'

Me too, thought Sarah. He doesn't know what he's taking on!

She set the juniors to tidying beds before the visitors, while she went round with the post-cibum medicines. They had just finished when the first visitor arrived and made a beeline for his wife.

'Sid!' called Mrs Dewhurst. 'I hope you haven't taken time off work?'

'Where on earth is my Bob?' asked May Greenwood, looking very smart in her outdoor clothes, and clutching a large holdall. 'He promised not to be late. If he's stopped off at the pub . . .'

A crowd of visitors came in all together, and in the middle of them Sarah could make out the reassuring figure of Mrs Priestley. A tall young soldier of about twenty, looking very sheepish, was walking beside her.

'Jim!' Even from the other end of the ward Samantha had seen him. She couldn't wait for him to arrive, but ran down the ward and threw her arms around the embarrassed young man. Mrs Priestley looked around nervously.

'Why don't you go in the side-ward?' said Sarah helpfully, taking hold of Mrs Priestley's arm and guiding her towards the door. 'It will be easier to talk in there.'

Mrs Priestley flashed her a grateful smile, and beckoned her son to follow her. Still clinging to her beloved Jim, Samantha went into the side-ward.

'Is it possible for me to have a word with the doctor, Nurse?' Mrs Priestley looked anxious.

'Of course—I'll give him a ring. How did you get on with Mrs Brown?' she asked tentatively.

'Oh, she's washed her hands of the whole affair . . .'

'Good,' interrupted Samantha.

'As far as she's concerned, I'm Samantha's mum now. Which suits me fine, because I can get on and help Jim with the wedding arrangements. It'll only be a small do, but still, there's a lot to see to, you understand . . .'

'I'll get the doctor,' said Sarah. That woman is a saint! she thought. She went off to phone the switchboard, leaving Mrs Priestley to cope with her newly enlarged family.

Dr Simmonds arrived on the ward a few minutes later, looking tired and impatient.

'So what's the problem, Nurse Williams?' he began without preamble.

'It's Samantha Brown, Doctor. Her boy-friend and his mother have come to take her home . . .'

'But I'm going to see them in Outpatients' next week, Nurse. It's all arranged!'

'The mother needs reassuring.' Sarah was surprised at the positive tone in her own voice.

John Simmonds raised his eyebrows disparagingly. 'Don't try to teach me how to run my own department, Nurse,' he snapped, testily. 'Stick to your nursing duties and don't overstep the mark—at least, not with me, anyway.'

'They're in the side-ward if you wish to see them, sir.' Sarah turned away from the hostile searching of his eyes and hurried away down the ward.

'Can you put these in water for me, Nurse?' called one of the visitors.

'Of course.' Sarah took the bouquet of flowers and made for the sluice. It would have been easy to hand the task over to a junior, but she wanted something nice and simple to occupy her until that high-handed Registrar had gone.

She was back at the desk signing certificates when Mrs Priestley, Samantha and Jim came to say goodbye.

'I can't thank you enough, Nurse. You've been so good to Sam,' said Mrs Priestley, smiling.

'I hope all goes well for you,' Sarah said.

'I'll come in and see you next week,' Samantha promised. 'I've got to see Dr Simmonds.'

'Such a nice man, isn't he?' added Mrs Priestley. 'So helpful.'

'Oh, absolutely!' Sarah agreed, smiling to herself. 'See you next week.' She turned, to see to the next visitor.

At the end of visiting, Sarah went round all the post-operative patients, checking drips, drainage tubes, packs, charts and dressings. There was just time to write up a report before Sister breezed in on the dot of five.

'You look nice, Sister,' Sarah said, admiring the new shorter hair-style.

Angela Dawson looked pleased. 'Do you think so, Nurse Williams? You don't think it's a bit . . . er . . . a bit daring?'

'I think it makes you look much younger, Sister.'

Bless the girl! She always did say the right things. 'Any problems, Nurse?' Sister asked brusquely.

'No, Sister. Would you like the report now?'

'Of course.'

They stood at the desk, Sister's eyes scanning the ward for any sign of laxity, while she listened to Sarah's voice.

'Thank you, Nurse Williams. I hope you have a nice evening. Are you going anywhere?'

'Just home to the children, Sister,' replied Sarah, surprised at the friendly approach.

'Yes, of course. Goodbye, Nurse.' Silly of me to forget the poor girl is a widow, thought Angela Dawson. She looks very tired. I hope it won't be too much for her. She'll make an excellent Sister one day.

Sarah went across to the changing room and changed into mufti. It was chilly as she made her way across the car park. She glanced idly at the front of the car as she unlocked the door, and her heart sank. One of the front tyres was flat. Opening the boot, she reached in for the spare wheel and hauled it out on the tarmac. Tools, that's what I need . . . She returned to peer inside the boot.

'Can I help you?' Alan Walker's friendly face was looking down at her.

She smiled with relief. 'I think I've got a puncture. Do you know anything about cars, Dr Walker?'

'Call me Alan, please.'

'And I'm Sarah,' she said, suddenly feeling very shy.

'I don't know much about cars, Sarah, but I can change a wheel.'

'Thank goodness for that, because I'm sure I can't.'

'Have you got a tool kit?' he asked.

'That's what I was just looking for . . . I've got one somewhere—yes, here it is.' Sarah triumphantly produced the greasy-looking bag and watched while Alan set about unscrewing the bolts.

Within seconds the flat tyre lay on the tarmac, and Alan was screwing the spare wheel into position.

'You'd better get that checked for tyre pressure when you fill up with petrol, but it should be all right for a few miles,' he told her, standing up and wiping his hand on a dirty rag.

'Here, let me find you a tissue,' said Sarah, rummaging in her bag. 'I can't seem to find one—here you are, use this.'

He wiped his hands absently on the hanky, then glanced down concernedly at the delicate lace edge. 'You shouldn't have given me this, Sarah. It's much too good—look what a mess I've made!'

'Not to worry. It'll wash.'

'I'll get my landlady to do it,' he said, pocketing the grimy handkerchief. 'That'll give her something to wonder about,' he added, with a mischievous grin.

Sarah laughed; he really was a pleasant young man— so fresh and uncomplicated.

'How about a drink?' he was asking. 'I know I could do with one. Leave the car here and we'll pop across to the Black Bull.'

She glanced at her watch.

'It's OK, they open at five-thirty, Sarah!'

'That's not what I was worrying about,' she smiled.
'I've got to get back. The family are expecting me.'

'One little drink won't take long. Come on.' He took
hold of her arm, and she allowed herself to be guided
across the busy road.

The landlord of the Black Bull was just opening up.

'What's the matter, Dr Walker? Can't you wait for
your pint this evening?' he asked with a broad smile, as
he went behind the bar. 'Haven't seen you in here
before, miss. Are you a new recruit?'

'Something like that,' she replied as she settled herself
on a bar stool.

'What will you have, Sarah?' Alan asked.

'I'd like an orange juice.'

'Don't you want anything stronger?'

'Not when I'm driving!'

'Just one?' he persisted.

'No . . . just one leads to another one. I used to
work on orthopaedics and I've seen too many drink-
driving casualties.' She was smiling but firm in her
refusal.

'I'm sure you're right,' he conceded. 'But I'll have a
pint of cooking, Fred.'

'Coming up, Doctor.'

'I really am most grateful,' she told Alan, as she
sipped her drink.

'It was a pleasure, to help a damsel in distress,' was his
gallant reply.

She smiled at him, and he thought how pretty she
looked out of uniform.

'You know, you ought to get out more often,' he told
her. 'You know what they say, all work and no play . . .'

'It's a bit difficult, Alan; you see, I've got the family to
think about.'

'I know all about that,' he said quietly.

'Ah, been checking up on me, have you?' Sarah tried to sound lighthearted.

'It would do you good to relax more,' he countered.

'Yes, Doctor,' she smiled, and finished off her drink.

'Another fruit juice?' he asked hopefully.

'No, thanks; I really must dash—I'm late as it is.'

'OK, but you must arrange to come out with me one evening when you've got more time. I won't give you the hanky back until you do,' he teased, waving it in front of her.

Sarah threw her head back and laughed, but her laughter froze as she saw the door opening. John Simmonds was coming across the bar towards them. He looked different without his hospital coat. Her heart began to pound.

'Enjoying yourselves?' he asked with a sardonic smile, his eyes taking in the lacy handkerchief in Alan's hand.

'Just relaxing, sir, after a hard day at the coal-face,' Alan told him.

'A good description,' agreed the Registrar. 'That's what it seemed like today. I haven't stopped for a minute. I didn't even have time for lunch. What will you have?' His invitation included both of them.

'I'll have another pint, sir, but I think Sarah's got to go,' said Alan.

'Sarah's got to go, has she?' John Simmonds reiterated derisively.

She flinched as he pronounced her name for the first time. 'The trials and tribulations of the working mother,' he added, fixing her with an amused smile. 'If that's where your duty lies, then you must go.'

'I'll have another fruit juice.' She surprised everyone including herself, as she changed her mind.

John Simmonds smiled his most charming smile. 'Of course you will, my dear—it's good to relax at the end of the day.'

'That's just what I was telling her, sir,' put in Alan.

I bet you were, thought the Registrar, eyeing the young houseman thoughtfully. Definite signs and symptoms of an imminent love affair . . . 'Let's dispense with the formalities when we're off duty, Alan. Call me John.'

'Yes, sir . . . I mean yes, John.'

Sarah laughed, aware of John Simmonds' searching eyes upon her. It was such an artificial situation, sitting here making polite conversation with a man who criticised her continually.

'Have you done something to your hair, Sarah?' The name sounded so strange, coming from him.

'I've had it cut.'

'Yes, it was long when you first arrived.'

What an observant man! Must be his medical training. 'I find it easier to manage like this.'

'I preferred it long,' John Simmonds said casually.

She turned her head; it had nothing to do with him how she did her hair . . . Funny, Mark always preferred her hair long . . . She shivered.

John Simmonds was ordering a sandwich. 'Anyone else?' he asked.

'No, thanks,' was the simultaneous reply.

'I'm starving!' The Registrar tucked in to his sandwich as if he had been away on a desert island.

Sarah watched him, and a strange feeling of compassion stole over her. He looked the sort of man who needed a woman to look after him. She noticed the cuff of one of his shirts was frayed. Wherever his absent wife was, she had not yet been replaced.

'I must go,' she said quickly.

John Simmonds put out his hand to help her down from the stool, and for a brief moment his long tapering fingers closed around hers before he released her.

'Have a good rest, Sarah. You look tired,' said the Registrar, in a gentle tone she hadn't heard before.

'I will. Goodbye, gentlemen!' She made for the door. So good for the morale, she thought bitterly, to be told I look tired, and I look better with long hair! Still, John Simmonds had not been at all overbearing just now—quite the reverse.

She climbed into her car and drove out through the hospital gates. The six o'clock traffic was piling up outside the Town Hall. It was a fine evening; the children would be playing out in Joanna's garden, so they wouldn't mind if she was a bit late, but even so . . . She inched the car forward. It was half an hour before she was clear of the town.

'Mummy!' The children came running across the garden to meet her. It was good to be back. 'Can we stay until we've finished our game?'

'Come and have a cup of tea,' called Joanna from the back door.

'Thanks, I will. Just a few more minutes, children . . .'

'Goody!' David ran back up the garden, followed closely by Fiona.

'Had a good day, Sarah?' asked Joanna, as the two friends drank their tea.

'Very satisfying,' Sarah said. 'I think I'm getting the hang of things at last.'

'Good. I thought it wouldn't take you long. Did you have to work late again?'

'Well, no; actually I had a flat tyre. One of the doctors changed it for me, and then we went off for a drink at the Black Bull,' Sarah admitted sheepishly.

'A cosy little twosome, eh?' Joanna had a broad grin on her face.

'No, it wasn't like that at all,' Sarah gabbled hastily. 'Our Registrar came in and joined us . . .'

'Did he indeed! The plot thickens,' laughed Joanna. 'Honestly, Sarah, I'm proud of you; you're behaving like a human being again.'

Sarah shot her a puzzled glance. 'What do you mean, Jo?' she asked.

'Well, you've been walking around like a zombie ever since Mark died. Three years is a long time. You ought to go out more often, meet people—especially eligible doctors!'

'Oh no, you don't,' Sarah said lightly. 'Don't start trying to matchmake, Joanna. I'm not interested in men any more—and especially doctors I have to work with. Dr Simmonds, our Registrar, is insufferable; besides, he's got some kind of hang-up about women. He definitely dislikes me. I think he's got a bitchy wife somewhere—perhaps I remind him of her.' She gave a hoarse little laugh.

'And how about the other one—the one who changed your tyre?'

'Alan Walker? He's quite good fun, really, I suppose, if you like that type. I think he's something of a hospital Romeo where the nurses are concerned.'

'But not your type, Sarah?'

'I didn't say that, exactly.'

'It's good to see your eyes shining again,' laughed Joanna. 'Quite like old times.'

'Where's Brian?' asked Sarah, quickly changing the subject.

'He's upstairs, trying to get some marking done. He works so hard, and yet we're hard up all the time. I wish I could go back to work again to help out, but he won't hear of it. Between you and me and the gatepost, he's looking around for another job.'

'He's not thinking of leaving teaching, is he?' Sarah asked in surprise.

'Not exactly,' replied Joanna mysteriously.

'Mummy, Christopher's fallen off the swing!'

Both mothers ran out into the garden. Christopher was sitting on the grass, rubbing his head and howling loudly. Joanna picked him up and examined him.

'Only a scratch, darling,' she soothed, cradling the little boy against her. The crying ceased. If it was only a scratch he might as well get on with the game . . . Christopher began to struggle out of his mother's arms, but she held him firmly.

'Oh no, you don't! Playtime's over for today. It's time for your bath.'

'Yes, we must be off now. Come along, children,' called Sarah, gathering up their belongings.

They drove home to the farm in the gathering dusk. Henry Gibson flung wide the door to welcome them. He had been watching anxiously for their return.

'At last!' he said happily. 'I thought you'd got lost.'

'No, I had a flat tyre, Dad—one of the doctors had to change it for me.'

He gave her a quizzical look, but made no further comment.

'Where's Grandma?' asked David.

'She's gone to bed early.'

'Again?' queried Sarah. This wasn't like her mother.

'Yes, I think she's a bit off colour. I've been telling her to see the doctor, but you know what she's like, lass.'

As stubborn as a mule, thought Sarah grimly. I'll take a look at her myself, and find out what's wrong, as soon as we have some time together.

'Come on children, bathtime . . . yes, of course I'll read you a story.'

Sarah found it difficult to concentrate on the story book. It wasn't just that she was tired. Perhaps Joanna was right—she had changed. There were strange new feelings stirring inside her. The touch of those long, tapering fingers had shaken her more than she dared to admit. Had she really been like a zombie for the past three years? She certainly didn't feel like a zombie now. Life suddenly seemed exciting again. She found herself looking forward to tomorrow.

CHAPTER SIX

THE next two days were uneventful, in terms of hospital life. Thursday found Sarah preparing the new Theatre cases, and on Friday she was busy with their post-operative care. When she went off duty in the evening she felt well satisfied with her first week back. There had been no further confrontations with the irascible Dr Simmonds—in fact he had been quite pleasant to her.

Sister, bless her, had given Sarah a weekend off.

'I think it's important for you to spend some time with your children, Sarah,' she said kindly. She had taken to calling Sarah by her first name when they were in the side-ward, out of earshot of the patients. Sarah wondered if she dared call Sister Angela, in return, but the idea seemed preposterous! 'But make sure you have a good rest, too,' Sister added firmly. 'I want you to be full of health and strength on Monday.'

'Yes, of course—thank you, Sister.' Sarah put on her cape and went out into the corridor. She was happy at the prospect of a whole weekend with David and Fiona, not to mention little sister Julie.

She walked quickly towards the front door.

'Coming to the dance tomorrow?'

Sarah swung round to see Alan Walker hurrying to catch up with her.

'No, I'm going to spend the weekend with the family,' she replied with a smile.

'All weekend?' he queried persistently.

'Yes, all weekend,' she repeated, smiling up at the fair-haired houseman.

'What a waste!' he said, with a charming grin. 'Don't worry—I'll make a date with you one of these days.'

72

She laughed. 'Goodbye, Alan—have a nice weekend.'

'And you, Sarah.' He watched the trim, attractive figure move off down the corridor.

I bet he's watching me, she thought. I definitely don't want to go out with him, but it's nice to be asked. Makes me feel like a woman again.

Julie was waiting for her in the foyer of the Nurses' Home.

'Come along, Sis, get a move on; we'll never get through the traffic at this rate,' she said, thinking how well her sister looked in her staff nurse's uniform.

'Give me a chance—I've only just got off duty! Some of us have to work, you know, not sit around a classroom all day!'

'I'll be jolly glad to get out of the classroom, I can tell you . . . Oh, I got nineteen out of twenty for the digestive system.'

'Not bad,' commented Sarah.

'Not bad! It was brilliant.'

'What happened to the other mark?' Sarah ducked as Julie pretended to throw her bag at her. 'Come through to the changing room; I won't be a minute, Julie.'

They managed to dodge the worst of the traffic and were soon speeding along the country road towards Riversdale.

'So you'll be glad to get on the wards, then,' Sarah queried.

'No—I shall be scared stiff. I'd just like to get out of PTS and away from those awful Sister Tutors,' Julie replied with feeling.

Not a very promising start to a nursing career, thought Sarah, as she drove gently past a herd of cows, on their way home to be milked. The herdsman waved to them. Sarah remembered him from the village school years ago, and waved back.

They collected the children from Joanna and arrived home just as their father was pulling off his boots, outside the back door. His face wrinkled into a happy smile.

'Hello, children!' he called.

'He means all of us,' whispered Julie, getting out of the car. She tipped her seat forward and lifted David and Fiona out.

'Grandpa!' They ran across the farmyard to give him a kiss.

Mrs Gibson had set out the tea on the kitchen table. Everything was homemade—bread, scones, cakes, jam, and even the cheese.

'Wow, that looks good, Mum,' said Julie, as she kissed her mother on the cheek.

'Sit yourselves down, then,' said Mrs Gibson, presiding over the teapot at the head of the table.

Sarah washed the children's hands at the kitchen sink, before joining the others. David sat on one side of her, and Fiona on the other. There was another snowy white tablecloth on the table. Sarah wished her mother wouldn't change the cloth every day, the children were sure to spill something, but that was the way her mother was made . . . You've got to set your standards, she always told Sarah.

She spread some damson jam on the fresh-baked bread and put it on Fiona's plate.

'Can I have some fruit cake, Mum?' asked the little girl, ignoring the bread.

'Bread before cake,' said Mrs Gibson, just as she had always said to her own children. 'And it's "may I have", not "can I have".'

Here we go again! thought Sarah.

When the meal was over she helped her mother with the washing up, while Julie took the children into the field.

'You're looking tired, Mum,' Sarah said worriedly.

'Am I, dear? Well, it's not surprising, what with the haymaking and everything else.'

'You ought to see Dr Baker for a check-up,' Sarah persisted.

'Perhaps,' said her mother vaguely. 'Just look at those children!' she exclaimed, opening the kitchen window. 'Julie, bring them out of that field—your father's only just started that one.' She banged the window shut. 'Honestly, Sarah, I sometimes think David has more sense than his Auntie Julie! And as for training to be a nurse . . . well!' Words failed her.

Sarah put the children to bed as soon as possible, sensing that her parents were tired. If it was fine tomorrow she would take them out for the day; perhaps take a picnic.

Fortunately, the day dawned sunny and warm. It was one of those late September days which made you think that spring was just around the corner, instead of six months away. Sarah jumped out of bed and flung the window open. She could hear the contented mooing of the cows in the mistle, where her father and his herdsman were milking. There was the smell of dew on the new-mown hay over in the field. Mm, it was good to be alive on a day like this. She put on her dressing-gown and tripped lightly down the stairs.

Her mother was sitting at the kitchen table, staring listlessly straight in front of her.

'What's the matter, Mum?' asked Sarah, sitting down beside her.

Mrs Gibson made no reply, as she pushed the newly arrived letter towards Sarah. It was an official letter from the Bradfield General. Its message was simple.

'A bed has been arranged for you at the Hospital for Women . . .'

Sarah looked at her mother in amazement. 'What's this all about, Mum?'

'I went to see Dr Baker last week, and he sent me to

see this specialist—Mr Shaw, I think his name was. He wants me to have a hysterectomy.'

'Just like that? Out of the blue, Mum? But what's the trouble?'

'I've been having this discharge, and I thought it would clear up . . .'

'But have you had a cervical smear?'

For a moment the older woman looked puzzled, then the light dawned. 'Oh, yes, I think they did one at the hospital,' she said.

'And is that the first one you've ever had taken?' Sarah asked in dismay.

'I'm not one of these people who's always bothering the doctor about something and nothing,' her mother retorted.

'Oh, Mum!' exclaimed Sarah in exasperation. 'If only women would realise the importance of regular cervical smears!'

Joan Gibson's weary face sagged, and she began to sob quietly. In the whole of her life Sarah had never seen her mother cry. Her mother was always the strong one in the family, the backbone, the one who always put herself last, and never had time for the frills of life. She put her arms round her and said,

'Don't worry, Mum; I'll look after you . . . Let's have a look—when do they want you to go in?'

Good Lord! . . . A week on Monday; this must be urgent. Sarah planned to have a chat with Mr Shaw as soon as possible, but she didn't want to alarm her mother.

'That's nice, Mum—you'll be on Nightingale Ward,' Sarah told her, feeling more than a little apprehensive, but her mother made no reply. She seemed to be in a state of shock. 'I'll make you a cup of tea, Mum.' It was the only thing she could think of, for the moment.

There was a noise on the stairs, as the children came hurtling down.

'Where are your slippers?' scolded Grandma.

That's a good sign! Sarah thought, as she warmed the earthenware teapot. Mum can't be feeling too bad.

Mrs Gibson put the letter away in her apron pocket and started to move around the kitchen, preparing the breakfast.

'I can do that, Mum. Why don't you go back to bed and have a lie-in?' Even as she said it Sarah knew what the response would be. Mrs Gibson had never gone back to bed in the whole of her life, and she wasn't going to start now.

When breakfast was over, Sarah suggested a picnic lunch. It would get the children out of the house, and leave her mother in peace for a while. The suggestion was greeted with wild enthusiasm by David and Fiona.

'Can Auntie Julie come too, Mum?' cried David.

'If she wants to,' replied Sarah cautiously. Her sister had not yet put in an appearance; she was probably still asleep.

'Let's go and ask her!' The children were halfway up the stairs before she could stop them. Oh well, Mum didn't like her daughters to stay in bed, so it was time Julie got up.

It was mid-morning before the picnic expedition was under way. The food was packed in the boot; the bag of bathing suits, buckets and spades, balls, rug to sit on, and towels had also been squeezed in beside the tool kit. David and Fiona were bobbing up and down on the back seat.

'Sit down, before I start the engine,' ordered Sarah sternly, making a mental note to have seat-belts fitted in the back as soon as possible. She turned to her sister. 'OK, Julie?'

'I think so. I'm not properly awake yet. Honestly, anyone would think we were setting off to climb Mount Everest, instead of nipping down to the river!'

Sarah laughed, 'You wait till you've got children of

your own! They always need so much paraphernalia.'
She started the engine and they moved off.

Mr Gibson waved to them from the hayfield. 'Goodbye, children.'

'Goodbye, Grandpa!'

The little red car turned down the hill towards the
river, and a few minutes later they were walking along
the footpath to their picnic spot. David was carrying his
new dinghy and the pump to blow air into it. Sarah had
not been too keen to bring it, but Grandpa, who had
bought the thing in the first place, had tied a rope to one
end, so that someone could always hold on to it in the
water. Fiona had the rug draped round her little
shoulders, while Sarah and Julie carried the rest of the
things.

'I feel like a refugee,' said Julie.

'What's a refugee, Auntie?' David asked.

Sarah was glad Julie was with her to help with the
children. It's so much easier when there are two of you,
she thought wistfully, suddenly remembering the picnics
she had had when the children were very small. That's
the first time I've thought about Mark today. I must be
getting better!

They settled themselves at the side of the river on a
stretch of sand and pebbles. The children got their
buckets and spades and started to dig.

'It's as good as being at the seaside here.' Julie leaned
back contentedly on the rug and turned her face to the
sun.

'It's better,' Sarah said, as she joined her sister. 'There
are no crowds. Mm, isn't it peaceful!'

Apart from the happy cries of the children, the only
other sounds were the rushing water, the birds, and the
occasional mooing of a cow. The two sisters sunbathed
in companionable silence, keeping a watchful eye on the
children nearby. At lunchtime they spread cold chicken
and salad on a cloth beside the rug, and everyone tucked

in. Sarah insisted on a short rest for the children before she allowed them to dash off and play again.

'Can I blow my dinghy up, Mum?'

'I'll do it, David,' Sarah said, reaching for the pump.

'Do you want me to take him out in it, Sarah?' asked Julie.

'Yes, please—but hold on to the rope. The current is very strong in the middle; don't go too far out.'

'Will you help me with my castle, Mummy?' asked Fiona.

'In a minute, dear. Let me finish this dinghy,' Sarah said, working away on the hand-pump.

When it was ready she watched anxiously as Julie waded into the water, taking David with her in the dinghy.

'OK, show me your castle,' she said, turning her attention to the little girl.

Several yards downstream, a man was walking towards them on the riverside path. He paused for a moment to watch the young mother and her daughter gathering pebbles to make a pattern on the sandcastle.

What a charming scene, he thought, then he screwed up his eyes in the strong sunlight, so as to get a better look. It couldn't be! Oh, yes, it was . . . No mistaking that trim attractive figure and the chic new hairstyle.

John Simmonds turned and decided to retrace his steps. As he did so, Fiona, tiring of working on the sandcastle, picked up the coloured ball and threw it towards her mother.

'Catch, Mummy!'

Sarah turned quickly, but the ball sailed past her into the river.

'Auntie Julie, get my ball, please,' called Fiona.

'No!' cried Sarah, as she saw Julie's automatic re-action was to leave go of the rope, as she reached for the ball.

Quick as a flash Julie turned back, but it was too late. The strong current had whipped the dinghy towards the middle of the river and was bearing it away downstream.

'Sit tight, David! I'm coming!' Sarah called, sprinting off down the path.

'I'll get him!' shouted a masterful voice, and Sarah had a blurred vision of a tall man in immaculate trousers wading out into the middle of the fast-flowing river to retrieve the dinghy. As he turned, she gave a gasp.

'Dr Simmonds! Thank you very much, sir. What a good thing you were here just now . . .'

In her embarrassment and relief that David was safe, she babbled on incessantly, extremely conscious of the dreadful state of his sodden, expensive trousers. He was pulling the dinghy up on to the sand, talking soothingly to the white-faced David. When he turned to face Sarah, his own face was very severe.

'Yes, it was a good thing I was here,' he said sternly. 'Don't you know those things are very dangerous?'

'Of course I do!' Sarah's relief had turned to anger.

Julie came running up. 'I'm sorry, Sarah; I only let go for an instant, and he was gone.' She stared up at the handsome stranger. 'Thanks very much—gosh, look at your trousers!'

John Simmonds glanced down at his wet legs, and smiled. 'It doesn't matter—they'll dry.'

'Yes, but you can't walk around in wet clothes—you'll catch your death,' cried Julie. 'I'm a nurse, so I should know.'

'Really?' said the doctor, grinning mischievously over her head to look at the elder sister.

Sarah opened her mouth to say something, but John Simmonds was enjoying himself.

'What a stroke of luck,' he said to Julie. 'So what do you think I should do, Nurse?'

'Well, take them off, of course,' Julie replied, without hesitation, then coloured with embarrassment. 'We live just up the road,' she continued hurriedly. 'I'm sure my father can lend you a pair?'

'Julie . . .' began Sarah, looking daggers at her little sister, but the doctor was fully in control of the situation.

'How very kind,' he said. 'My car is up there by the side of the road, Miss . . . er . . . ?'

'Gibson . . . but you can call me Julie.'

'And you can call me John.'

'OK, John. Just follow behind us, will you—it's not far.'

Sarah squirmed. Just wait till I get her into the car! she muttered to herself.

David had fully recovered from his ordeal, and chatted away happily to the kind man who had saved him.

'When I grow up I'm going to have a real boat,' he said importantly. 'I've got a battleship at home. Would you like to see it?'

'I would indeed.' John Simmonds smiled at the little boy, as he helped the girls to gather up their picnic things.

Julie, too, talked non-stop to the charming stranger, and couldn't understand why her sister was so quiet.

They made their way back to the road, and David gave a whistle of admiration when he saw the blue Mercedes.

'What a fantastic car! Can I have a ride in it?'

'Of course you can,' said John Simmonds, opening the back door.

'Me too!' cried Fiona, scrambling in beside her brother.

'It's OK, Mum,' said John Simmonds solemnly. 'It's fitted with childproof doors.'

The little convoy moved off towards Riversdale. Sarah glanced in her driving mirror to see if he was following her.

'I say, Sarah, I hope it's safe to let the kids go with that man,' said Julie. 'I mean, he looks all right—positively gorgeous, in fact—but we don't know anything about him, do we?'

'We do,' said Sarah drily. 'He's a Gynae Registrar.'

'Is that important?' asked Julie.

'Oh, Julie!' Sarah couldn't help but laugh at her little sister. 'Let's say I find it somewhat embarrassing taking the great man home to change his trousers. I've got to work with him, you know . . .'

'Yes, but I couldn't let the poor man stay in his wet things all day, could I?'

They pulled into the farmyard. Mrs Gibson looked out of the window, hastily removing her working pinafore when she saw the smart car.

'This is Dr Simmonds,' began Sarah, as her mother opened the door.

'Whatever happened to you?' cried the startled Mrs Gibson. 'Come inside, will you, and let me have a look.'

'Dr Simmonds went in the river to catch the dinghy,' Julie explained. 'I thought he'd better change out of his wet things.'

'Quite right, Julie,' said her mother. 'He's got very long legs, though, hasn't he? I think your father's trousers will be too short, but I've got a pair of Michael's old cricket flannels. Come with me, Doctor; I'll soon fix you up.'

As John Simmonds followed Mrs Gibson upstairs, Sarah marvelled at the way her mother took everything in her stride.

'Put the kettle on,' called Mrs Gibson from the top of the stairs. 'You'll need something to warm you up, Doctor. However did it happen . . .'

The voice was lost on the landing. Sarah turned to her sister and smiled.

'I just don't believe this is happening,' she said, in a bemused state. John Simmonds wandering around the house with her mother!

'He's in the bathroom, changing,' Mrs Gibson

announced when she returned. 'Such a nice man. He says you work together?'

'Yes; he's Mr Shaw's Registrar.'

'Well, he's very pleasant. Is he married?'

'I'm sure I don't know,' Sarah replied truthfully.

'Is the kettle boiling, Julie? Put this clean cloth on, Sarah. Thank goodness I baked this morning!' Mrs Gibson darted round the kitchen, organising her daughters. 'Sarah, wash the children's hands, Dr Simmonds will be down in a minute. Julie, go and call your father—he's in the top field.'

By the time Dr Simmonds came down the entire family was waiting for him at the table. He cast his eye over the farmhouse tea and smiled at Mrs Gibson.

'I do hope you haven't prepared this feast especially for me, Mrs Gibson.'

'Not at all, Doctor. We always have a good tea. Come and sit yourself down next to me,' she replied.

Sarah felt the brush of his sleeve, as he sat down between her and her mother. It was only the faintest contact, but it excited her. There was also a hint of expensive after-shave, as he moved beside her. He definitely didn't wear that in hospital; it would upset the patients, she thought—the nurses too! It's having a weird effect on me . . .

'Pass Dr Simmonds one of my scones, Sarah.'

Sarah complied, as if in a dream.

'Thank you, Sarah,' he said, wondering at the strange expression in her liquid brown eyes. It would be very easy to become attached to such a delightful girl, if only he weren't determined never to become involved again. He smiled at her, a slow, poignant smile, full of the emotional pain he had suffered.

Sarah was transfixed by those deep blue, sad eyes. She wanted to drown in them, and erase the unhappiness that lay beneath the surface of that suave façade.

'Pass the scones round, lass.' Her father's voice

brought her back to reality. Her legs, beneath the table, felt weak. She was desperately aware of that strong masculine thigh only inches away.

'David, just look at my tablecloth!' The moment passed as Sarah sprang to help her mother mop up the inevitable wet cloth.

'So, what brings you into the neighbourhood, Dr Simmonds?' asked Mr Gibson.

'I'm house-hunting, actually. I came out to look at a cottage on the other side of Riversdale, and I was having a walk by the river when I met your daughters.'

'I would have thought you'd need to be a bit nearer the hospital, Doctor, if you don't mind me saying so.'

'Oh, I've got a flat by the hospital, but I want somewhere quieter for weekends off and so forth.'

When the meal was finished, John Simmonds said he had to get back to hospital.

'But I haven't shown you my battleship,' David cried, jumping down from the table and scurrying away to his toy cupboard.

The Registrar stood up. 'I'd forgotten about that, David,' he said solemnly.

He really is a good-looking man, Julie was thinking. Even in Mike's old flannels he's very fanciable.

'Here it is!'

John Simmonds bent down and took the battleship in his strong, sensitive hands. 'This is a marvellous piece of engineering, David. Does it float?'

'You bet! Come on down to the pond and I'll show you . . .'

'David,' interrupted Sarah quickly, 'I don't think Dr Simmonds has time to . . .'

'That's all right. I'll make time, but only if you'll come down to the pond with us.'

To her dismay, she started to blush, so she hurried towards the door to conceal her embarrassment. 'Come along, David,' she muttered brusquely.

The dazzling rays of the afternoon sun were dancing on the pond in the field beyond the farmyard. David ran gleefully ahead clutching his precious ship. Sarah could sense that John's long legs had caught up with her, and she glanced shyly sideways. He was looking down at her with tenderness in his deep blue eyes. She took in the rugged bone structure of his face, the sensuous lips, the strong white teeth, and turned away with an inaudible sigh, unable to understand the confusion of her emotions.

Without warning, he took hold of her hand playfully, and cried, 'Come on, let's catch David!'

Together they ran over the springy turf down to the pond. David had already pushed the ship out on to the shallow water and was removing his shoes and socks. He looked up at the tall doctor and asked innocently, 'Do you want to paddle?'

John Simmonds laughed and bent down to untie his shoelaces.

'I shouldn't advise it,' said Sarah in alarm. 'It's rather muddy.'

'Nonsense! If it's OK for David it's OK for me.' He rolled up his trousers and waded into the pond. David clutched his hand, only letting go when it was necessary to steer the ship in a different direction.

Sarah sat on a warm stone, taking in the pleasant scene. She felt happier than she had done for a long time.

'I'm afraid I'll have to go back to the hospital,' John said after a few minutes, gently leading David back to the edge of the water. His eyes met Sarah's. 'You've got a wonderful son here. You're very lucky.'

Tears started to prick behind her eyelids, and she stood up quickly. 'Shall I carry the battleship?'

'No, I've got it, Mum.'

They walked back across the field, with David in between them. John got into his car and leaned out of the window. 'Say goodbye to your mother for me, and thank her for the lovely tea.'

She nodded, smiling, and turned away hurriedly. There was a strange empty feeling after he had gone. Sarah felt restless. The prospect of the whole weekend on the farm had palled . . . and she had been so looking forward to it.

CHAPTER SEVEN

THERE was a new batch of patients to be admitted on Monday morning. Sarah found herself hurrying from one to the other, in an attempt to get everyone settled in before Mr Shaw's round. Sister Dawson was off duty until one o'clock, so Sarah was in charge, with Staff Nurse Fielding assisting her. As the great man swept into the room, she went to meet him.

'Good morning, Staff,' he breezed. 'You're looking full of the joys of living this morning, my dear. Did you have a good weekend?'

Sarah was aware that all the eyes in Mr Shaw's entourage were upon her—especially those of Dr Simmonds.

'Very pleasant, sir,' she murmured, motioning to Nurse Crabtree to bring the notes trolley over. Nurse Fielding had started the dressings—good.

'So you're in charge this morning, I see.'

'Yes, sir.'

'Let's have a look at the Wertheim's case; Mrs Davis,' said Mr Shaw, moving across the ward with his followers close behind.

'Mrs Davis is making good progress, sir.' Sarah reached for the patient's file.

'Splendid . . . Good morning, Mrs Davis; how are we today?'

Mr Shaw listened intently to the favourable reply and nodded. 'Fine; well, if you continue like this we'll be able to send you home in about a week's time.'

He glanced at the charts Sarah had produced. 'How is the wound now, Staff?'

'It's clean, sir.'

'Good—keep up the good work. Goodbye, Mrs Davis.'

They moved on to the next patient, as the medical secretary scribbled in her notebook. She was new on the firm, rather younger than Mr Shaw's last secretary, with a tendency to get flustered over minor details, Sarah noticed.

'Shall I make arrangements for Mrs Davis's discharge, sir?' asked the hapless secretary nervously.

'Good Lord, no!' said the consultant. 'Our patients aren't battery hens, you know.' He paused for the inevitable polite laughter to die down. 'Anything can happen in a week—you have to take each case on its merit . . . Now, who have we here, Staff?'

The ward round seemed to take longer than usual, or perhaps it was simply that Sarah was conscious of the work load that had to be got through that morning. She was also aware of the constant proximity of the Registrar. However she tried, he always finished up standing behind her at the bedside. She could feel his breath on the back of her neck, and once, as she turned to move on, he seemed to linger just a little longer than was necessary. She looked up into the cool, enigmatic eyes; his lips were smiling at her, but the blue eyes remained sad.

As the procession made its way, finally, to the door, Sarah thought she had better offer the usual hospitality which was de rigueur for Sister Dawson.

'May I offer you a coffee, Mr Shaw?' she asked him.

'Thank you, my dear. I think we've time for a coffee, John, haven't we?'

The Registrar nodded. 'Just a quick one, sir, but Dr Walker had better see to that IV on Cavell.'

'And Jane must go and write up her scribblings before they go clean out of her head,' added Mr Shaw, turning to his blonde secretary. 'So it's just two of us for coffee, Staff—and your good self, of course.' The students didn't count. They hadn't yet served their time.

As Sarah followed the consultant and his Registrar into the side-ward, she felt a hand on her arm.

'This is yours,' Alan Walker whispered, thrusting the lacy handkerchief into her hand.

She smiled up at the fair-haired houseman. 'You shouldn't have bothered to have it washed . . .' she began, then saw that John Simmonds was holding the door open for her. His severe look told her that he hadn't missed anything.

'What time are you off today, Sarah?' persisted Alan Walker.

'There is a patient waiting for you on Cavell, Dr Walker,' barked the Registrar.

'Yes, *sir*.' Alan put slightly too much emphasis on the 'sir', before hurrying away.

There's no love lost between those two, thought Sarah, as she walked in front of John Simmonds.

The consultant and the Registrar ignored Sarah as she made the coffee, which was just as well, because she was feeling decidedly nervous. Sister Dawson always put the coffee percolator on, but Sarah hadn't time for such luxury this morning. They would have to make do with instant.

'Coffee, gentlemen?' Sarah stood beside Mr Shaw's chair. She had put the instant coffee into Sister's blue coffee pot, and it looked quite respectable.

'Thank you, my dear,' said Mr Shaw absently, and continued his conversation.

'How are the children?' asked John Simmonds, suddenly turning his attention away from the chief.

'Very well.' Sarah was surprised at the sudden attention.

'You have children?' Mr Shaw's eyes were wide with amazement. 'And what does hubby do for a living?'

'I'm a widow. My husband was a doctor.'

'I'm sorry, my dear, I had no idea. You said last week you lived on a farm, I remember.'

'Yes, I live with my parents. Actually, sir,' this was as good a time as any to broach the subject of her mother, she thought, 'I wonder if you could spare me a few minutes some time. My mother came to see you in Outpatients, and she's coming in for a hysterectomy next week.'

'Come down to my office about two o'clock. I'll get my secretary to dig the notes out. What's your mother's name?'

'Joan Gibson, sir.'

Mr Shaw wrote the name in his notebook.

'More coffee, sir?'

'No, thank you, my dear. We must away.'

Both men stood up, and Sarah went towards the door.

'I'll see you at two, Staff Nurse,' said the consultant briskly. 'Now, about that hysterocolpectomy in intensive care, John . . .'

Sarah brushed against John Simmonds as he stood back to let her pass. He's not wearing that after-shave this morning, she thought, but he still makes my legs feel wobbly.

She went back into the ward and picked up the reins again. Nurse Crabtree was in floods of tears in the sluice, because she'd broken a thermometer and was afraid Sister would be angry.

'She was furious last time I broke something, Staff,' she sobbed. 'Threatened to have me moved to another ward; and I've got my exams coming up!'

'That's what it is,' said Sarah gently. 'Things always seem worse just before exams. Don't worry, I'll put in a good word for you.'

'Oh, will you really?' Nurse Crabtree brightened up.

'Yes, of course I will. Now go and start tidying the beds with Nurse Rothwell. It's almost lunchtime.'

Sister came back on duty promptly at one o'clock. She

looked relaxed and refreshed after her morning off, and listened with interest to every detail of Sarah's report. By contrast, she showed no interest at all in the broken thermometer.

'Pre-exam nerves, I expect,' she said dismissively.

'That's exactly what I told her, Sister.'

'Well, on your way, girl. I expect you're ready for some lunch.'

'I may be a few minutes late back, Sister. I've got to see Mr Shaw at two o'clock.'

'Nothing wrong, I hope?' Angela Dawson's voice was sympathetic.

'My mother's one of his patients—I'm hoping he'll fill me in on the details,' Sarah said briefly. Time enough to tell Sister her mother was going to be admitted to Nightingale when she knew more about it herself.

'Well, run along, then. I'll see you when you get back.'

Sarah collected her cape from the side-ward and made off down the corridor to the dining-room. As she ate her lunch, the thought uppermost in her mind was her mother's impending operation. It was unusual for the wheels to be set in motion so quickly, unless . . . She tried to dismiss her fears. Time enough to worry when she had seen Mr Shaw.

At five minutes to two, Sarah was standing outside Mr Shaw's office. Jane Worthing, on her way back from lunch, paused to smile at the friendly staff nurse, before unlocking the door.

'Come in, Nurse Williams. He's not here yet, thank goodness, but you can wait in here.'

The young secretary sat down at her desk and pulled out a powder compact. 'Is there anything I can do for you, Nurse?' she asked as she outlined her lips with shocking pink.

'No, thanks . . . except, you have got my mother's notes, haven't you?'

'Your mother? Oh, yes; that case Mr Shaw told me

about. I had to go and fetch them this morning . . . here
we are. Joan Gibson, suspected cervical carcinoma . . .
Oh, sorry; perhaps I should have waited for Mr
Shaw . . .'

'You certainly should have waited, Miss Worthing,'
said the consultant, coming through the open door and
fixing his secretary with a withering look. 'Come this
way, Staff Nurse.'

Sarah followed Mr Shaw into the inner sanctum. Her
fears were being confirmed . . . cervical cancer. If only
Mum had taken the time to go and have a smear test!

'Sit down here, Nurse Williams,' he said kindly. 'I'm
sorry you had to hear the provisional diagnosis from my
secretary.'

'That's all right, sir. I'd like to know all the details,
please,' Sarah told him, feeling miserable at the
prospect.

'Your mother was referred to me by her GP, a
Dr . . . ?'

'Dr Brown, sir.'

'Ah, yes, here it is, Dr Brown. A smear test was
carried out, and some malignant cells were revealed. I
therefore carried out a colposcopy to determine the
extent of the cancer. As far as I can tell at this stage, the
growth is confined to the uterus and the cervix, but an
immediate radical hysterectomy is indicated.'

'A Wertheim's operation, sir?'

'Exactly. It's an invasive carcinoma, you understand,
but if we move quickly we can prevent a lymphatic
spread.'

'And what's the prognosis, Mr Shaw?'

'Ah, that depends on the operation, my dear. I'm
afraid I can't tell you that at this stage. Only a gypsy with
a crystal ball could hazard a guess.' He smiled, but his
attempt at levity was lost on Sarah. If only . . .

As if reading her thoughts the consultant said, 'You
know, if I'd seen your mother six months ago, things

would have been different. The simple smear test reveals early histological changes which are not detected clinically. If it were possible to screen the entire population frequently enough, we could virtually eliminate cervical cancer. Well, don't be too depressed, young lady—we'll do all we can. There's just one other problem . . .'

'Yes?' Sarah asked quickly.

'Your mother's haemoglobin is very low. We'll have to give her some pre-operative blood transfusions to raise the level. I don't like operating when it's less than 10.2, so we must allow two weeks before operation.'

Sarah did a quick calculation. Two weeks before operation and then at least two weeks after—her mother would be in hospital for a minimum of a month.

'Thank you very much, Mr Shaw,' she said, standing up and preparing to go. 'How much does my mother know?'

'I've explained as well as I can to her, but one can never be sure how much the patient understands. As I recall, she didn't ask any questions.'

She wouldn't, thought Sarah. Mum would be too scared of making a nuisance to herself.

She turned and went into the outer office. Jane Worthing was hard at work on her typewriter, hoping to escape the wrath of her boss.

Back on the ward, Sister came hurrying to meet her.

'How did it go?' she asked quickly.

'My mother is going to be admitted next Monday, here on Nightingale, for a Wertheim's,' Sarah told her in a faraway voice that didn't sound like her own.

'Oh, my dear girl!' Sister was all concern.

'She's going to be in for a couple of weeks before operation because of her low haemoglobin.'

'Yes, well, we'll sort that out when the time comes.' Sister glanced anxiously at her staff nurse, wondering what domestic problems this was going to pose. And

much as she admired her, she couldn't allow the poor girl
to nurse her own mother. It would never work; there was
too much emotional involvement with a mother and
daughter. Angela Dawson resolved to speak to Matron.

'Are you feeling all right, Staff Nurse?'

'Yes, thank you, Sister. What would you like me to
do?'

'Medicines, please, and then take a look at Mrs
White's dressing; it needs changing.'

Sarah threw herself into her work, and there was no
time to brood. By the time she went off duty she had
come to terms with the situation.

When she got back to Riversdale, Joanna took
one look at her face and asked, 'What's the problem,
Sarah?'

Sarah smiled. 'Is it that obvious?'

'Certainly is. Come on, out with it!'

'Mum's going in for a Wertheim's. She'll be in at least
a month.'

'Sorry about that.' Joanna was quiet for a few moments, then she said quietly, 'How are you going to cope
at home?'

'I'm not sure—I haven't had time to think about it
yet.'

'When does she go in?'

'Next Monday, so there's not much time to sort things
out. I might be able to get Mrs Asquith from the village
to come in and clean.'

'Don't bother,' said Joanna, her voice suddenly becoming excited.

Sarah looked at her friend enquiringly.

'I've got a plan that will help us both,' Joanna explained. 'You remember I said that Brian was looking
for a new job—well, he's got it! He's going to teach
English as a foreign language in Saudi Arabia. They
want him to start in January, but he has to go on a course
first. It begins in London next week, and you know how I

hate being by myself. I was wondering if Christopher and I could move into the farm while he's away.'

'Why, of course, Jo,' Sarah replied breathlessly. A great weight seemed to have rolled away.

'I could look after your dad as well as the children,' Joanna was saying.

'And you'll be there all the time, which is how it should be,' added Sarah, then laughed. 'Oh, dear, I'm beginning to sound like Mum—the mother's place is in the home . . . but seriously, Jo, it will be great having you there, and we've plenty of room. You can have Anne's room—she won't be home till Christmas.' A sudden thought crossed her mind. 'Will you be going out to Saudi Arabia with Brian?'

'Not for the first three months, at least. He's supposed to settle in before his wife and family arrive.'

That means another arrangement when Joanna leaves Riversdale, thought Sarah. Oh well, I'll have to cross that bridge when I come to it.

'When does Brian go to London?' she asked.

'Sunday afternoon.'

'I'll have a room ready for you, then.' Sarah stood up. 'Come on, children—home-time!'

Mrs Gibson seemed more cheerful than she had done for a long time when they got back to the farm. Having faced up to her problem, she felt that she was now in good hands.

If they're all like that nice young doctor who came to tea, I shan't mind going in, she had told herself.

After she had put the children to bed, Sarah sat by the fire with her parents, drinking cocoa. No one spoke for a while; it was so quiet, you could hear the ticking of the grandfather clock. She was the first to break the silence.

'I saw Mr Shaw today, Mum.'

'Did you, dear; that was nice.'

Another long silence.

'Did you know you'll be in hospital for about a month?'

'Yes, dear; he told me. Did you ask Joanna for that recipe for cheesecake?'

I give up! Sarah thought. 'Yes, I did, Mum. Oh, by the way,' she began tentatively, 'Brian has to go to London on a course next week, so I've asked Joanna to come and stay here.'

'That was nice of you. I know she doesn't like being on her own,' said Mrs Gibson.

Mr Gibson gave his daughter a shrewd look. 'I suppose you thought I couldn't manage on my own, eh?' he muttered, with a knowing smile.

'Not at all, Dad, but the children are a bit of a handful. It will be nice for them to know there's a mum here all the time.'

Mrs Gibson gave a sniff, but refrained from making her favourite speech. This was no time to antagonise her daughter. She was going to need her help during the next few unknown weeks. The four children had been born at home, and it would be her first time in hospital.

'I'm going to bed now,' she said. 'What time are you on tomorrow?'

'Not till one o'clock, so I'll take the children to school. Good night, Mum.'

'Good night, dear. Don't be long, Henry.'

'I'm coming up, in a minute.' Henry Gibson waited until his wife was out of earshot before saying, 'She will be all right, your mother, won't she?'

'We'll do all we can for her, Dad. She'll be in the best place.'

'That's what I thought,' he said quietly. He stood up and knocked his pipe against the fire grate, before placing it in his pipe rack. 'Good night, Sarah.'

'Good night, Dad.'

She remained by the fire after he had gone upstairs,

listening to the ticking of the clock, and feeling decidedly lonely. The prospect of going to her narrow bed again seemed most uninviting. She found herself wondering what it would be like if there was someone to share her life with—other than the children—someone to care for intensely . . .

No, I couldn't! Unconsciously, Sarah shook her head, as she stood up and reached for the fireguard. There are too many memories haunting me.

Next morning as she stood by the school gate waving goodbye to the children, Sarah had forgotten the strange thoughts of the previous evening. She looked around at the other mums, smiling happily at their offspring, before returning to her little red car and shooting off back to the farm. The postman was just arriving.

'Parcel for your mother, Sarah,' he said, smiling genially. He had known young Sarah since she was knee-high to a grasshopper, and she hadn't changed a bit . . . no, not one little bit, even after all the poor lass had been through.

'That's nice, Sam,' said Sarah. 'I'll take it in, if you like.' She opened the kitchen door and disappeared.

Sam took his time getting back on his bike . . . sometimes there was a cup of tea going . . . not today, evidently.

'There's a parcel for you, Mum.'

'For me?' asked Mrs Gibson in surprise. 'It's not my birthday, is it?'

Sarah laughed. 'Open it up. Don't keep us in suspense!'

Mrs Gibson carefully undid the string, winding it methodically into a little ball, which she placed in a drawer.

'Hurry up, Mother,' said Mr Gibson. 'They're waiting for me out in yon field.'

His wife removed the brown paper. 'Why, it's from Dr Simmonds,' she exclaimed. 'It's Michael's flannels—

that was quick. And he's had them cleaned. Oh, look at this, Sarah!'

Wrapped in tissue paper was a box of expensive handmade chocolates.

'Now isn't that kind,' Mrs Gibson said. 'And there's a little card: "Thank you for a delicious tea." What a charming young man!'

How very thoughtful of him. It seemed to have cheered her mother immensely. Sarah started to clear away the breakfast things, her mind leaping ahead to one o'clock, when she would be on the ward again.

Sister Dawson greeted her rather too effusively when she arrived. She's up to something, thought Sarah. I wonder what it is.

She was left in no doubt, for as soon as the report was over Angela Dawson asked Sarah to go into the side-ward with her.

'I don't know quite how to put this, Sarah,' she said, closing the door behind them. 'The fact is I've asked for you to be transferred to another ward.'

Sarah stared at Sister Dawson in disbelief. 'But why, Sister? Aren't you satisfied with my work?'

'It's no reflection on you, Sarah, but I can't have one of my nurses taking care of her mother. Matron agrees with me; you would be too involved emotionally.'

So she'd been to see Matron already. They were probably right. 'I suppose it might be a strain,' Sarah conceded. 'But you will allow me to visit?'

'Of course, my dear—whenever you're free.' Sister felt relieved that Sarah had taken it so well.

'Where are you moving me to?' Sarah asked quietly.

'Matron thinks you should be away from the gynaecology wards altogether, so she's transferring you to Male Orthopaedic. I understand you spent several months on the ward during your training, and also Sister Stuart is a contemporary of yours.'

'Yes, we were in PTS together.'

'Well, that will be nice for you.'

'How long will I stay on Orthopaedics, Sister?' For some reason she felt anxious to return to Nightingale Ward as soon as possible.

'That will depend on your mother's progress,' replied Sister kindly. 'When she's discharged, I'll ask for you to be transferred back again.'

'Thank you.' She stood up and made her way back on to the ward. It would be pleasant working with Liz Stuart, but she was going to miss Nightingale, in more ways than one. The post-operative theatre cases kept her busy all afternoon, checking drips, taking blood pressures, relieving pain with the prescribed drugs when necessary, and generally giving reassurance to her patients.

'Would you like to go off for your tea-break, Nurse Williams?'

Sarah glanced at the clock. Four-thirty already! 'Yes, thank you, Sister.'

She wrapped her cape around her and hurried off down the corridor, anxious not to waste a second of her half hour. It was chilly when she left the Women's Hospital to walk the few yards to Bradfield General.

Liz Stuart was in her office on Male Orthopaedic. 'Sarah! What a nice surprise,' she said, opening the door to her friend. 'I hear you're coming over to us next week.'

'I'm glad they've told you, Liz,' said Sarah, sitting down by the desk. 'It's only temporary, of course, till Mum goes home.'

'So Matron explained to me; cup of tea?'

'Yes, please, I won't have time to go to the dining-room. You don't mind having me on the ward?'

'Of course not, silly; it will be just like old times.'

'Except you will be the Sister in charge.'

'And you will be a valuable member of the team. Now drink your tea, and don't make such a fuss . . . oh, guess what! I met that dishy Registrar of yours at Mr Thwaite's dinner party last night. He's taking me to the theatre on Saturday night . . . I was so surprised when he asked me—I mean, he's always so proper and correct. I think he's lonely, don't you?'

'Probably,' replied Sarah in a distant voice, wishing her heart would stop pounding.

'Anyway, I can't wait. I'm going to go out and blow my salary cheque on something exotic to wear. I mean, if he is free from his wife, he's quite a catch.'

Suddenly Sarah felt sorry she had come over to see Liz. More than anything else she wanted to get back to Nightingale. She drained her cup and stood up quickly.

'Got to go,' she said briefly.

'So soon?' Liz looked at her friend curiously.

'I mustn't be late back. I only wanted to see if you'd heard about my transfer. Goodbye.'

Sarah pulled her cape tightly round her and bent her head against the cold wind in the street.

'Hey, look where you're going!'

'Alan! Sorry, I didn't see you.' She almost collided into the arms of the houseman.

'You were miles away.' There was a broad grin on his good-looking face. 'Penny for them!'

'Not worth a penny,' she replied lightly.

'About that date, Sarah?'

'What date?' she asked, with a puzzled look.

'The date you promised me if I returned your hanky. Well, you've got it back.'

'I never promised anything of the sort,' Sarah laughed. 'You said that if . . .'

'OK, maybe I got it wrong,' he conceded, smiling down at her teasingly. 'But that doesn't prevent you coming out with me, now does it? There's a dance in the medics' hostel, and some of us qualified old men have been invited, to raise the tone of the occasion, I think, and I'd be delighted if you would come with me.'

'When is it?' she asked.

He looked surprised. So far so good. 'It's on Saturday night.'

Saturday night . . . Yes, she wanted to go out on Saturday night; anything was better than staying in, brooding about . . .

'OK. You've got yourself a date,' she said.

'Great! Can I pick you up?'

'Better not.' Sarah smiled as she thought of her mother's face, if she were to invite him out to Riversdale. 'I'll turn up on my own. What time?'

'About eight.'

'Fine . . . I'll be there. Goodbye.'

She hurried back to the ward, wondering what she'd let herself in for. It was only a bit of harmless fun, and everyone agreed she ought to go out more.

CHAPTER EIGHT

FOR the rest of the week, Sarah found herself rushed off her feet on Nightingale Ward. She had no time to think about her impending move to Orthopaedics, nor her mother's operation. Alan Walker had reminded her twice about their Saturday date at the medics' dance—once in front of John Simmonds. The Registrar gave Sarah a strange smile.

'Beginning to enjoy the hospital social life, are you, Sarah?' he asked.

It was the first time he had used her first name on duty; she glanced at him in surprise, but his deep blue, expressive eyes gave nothing away.

'I'm not exactly a recluse,' she snapped back, a little too bitterly.

He seemed surprised at her reaction. 'I never said you were. It's good for you nurses to relax in your off-duty.'

'So everyone keeps telling me,' she said quietly.

'You'd better take care of Sarah, on Saturday, Alan,' John Simmonds added mockingly. 'Girls like her are very vulnerable.'

Now what on earth does he mean by that? she mused angrily, moving away from the two doctors, to get on with her work.

'I can take care of myself,' she retorted, and winced as she saw the patronising smile on Dr Simmonds' face. Unfeeling brute! I'm glad I'm going to Male Orthopaedic . . . at least I won't have to put up with his cryptic remarks, she thought.

Sarah made a point of avoiding John Simmonds, but on Friday afternoon, during visiting hours, he caught up with her in the treatment room. She was in the act of removing a Ferguson's speculum from the steriliser, and the Registrar's unexpected arrival almost caused her to release the hold on her forceps.

'Sorry to startle you,' he began, with a boyish grin. 'Mrs Tate is asking for you on Psychiatric, and I wondered if you could spare a few minutes.'

Sarah placed the speculum in a sterile kidney dish and looked up at John Simmonds thoughtfully. He was obviously in a friendly mood today. She would try not to antagonise him too much.

'Mrs Tate? How is she, Doctor?'

'She's responding well to treatment, and appears lucid most of the time. Your diagnosis was correct, Nurse— persecution mania.'

Sarah refrained from saying, I told you so. He would definitely not approve of being reminded how he had snapped at her.

'When does she want to see me, Doctor?' she asked quietly.

'As soon as possible; I've asked Sister if you can be away from the ward for a few minutes, and she's quite agreeable.'

'Oh, well, it seems to be all settled, then.' She removed her sterile gown and rolled down her sleeves, carefully putting on the stiffly starched cuffs. 'Let's go, Dr Simmonds.'

He held open the door and they went out together into the ward. Some of the visitors glanced idly at the handsome doctor and the attractive staff nurse, thinking what a charming couple they made.

The Psychiatric Wing was on the top floor. Sarah moved quickly along the corridor, intensely aware of the tall figure at her side. The staff nurse on duty let them into Mrs Tate's room with a friendly smile. News of Sarah's involvement in the case had reached the Psychiatric Unit, and she was something of a heroine, although everyone was too professional to mention it.

'Nurse Williams!' cried Mrs Tate effusively, as they entered. She was sitting by her bed, looking very pretty in a pink silk dressing gown, with her hair newly washed by the hospital hairdresser. The room was full of flowers and cards. 'And Dr Simmonds, too. How nice of you both to come!'

Sarah smiled with happiness. 'You're looking wonderful, Mrs Tate.'

'I feel wonderful, Nurse. They've been so good to me here. I'm going home soon. But I wanted to see you before I went to thank you for all your help on . . .' she paused and glanced up at Dr Simmonds appealingly.

'On the night you were taken ill,' he supplied helpfully.

'Exactly.' The patient gave a relieved smile. 'I can't remember much about that evening, but I remember you were both very kind.'

'All in the line of duty, Mrs Tate,' said Sarah briskly.

'Maybe, but I shall never forget you both,' Mrs Tate added softly.

'We'll sort out your medication before you go, Mrs Tate.' John Simmonds wanted to complete the medical practicalities of the case. 'And then we shall want to see you in Outpatients, every week to begin with—can you manage that?'

'Of course, Doctor. It will be a pleasure to come back and see everybody.'

They said goodbye and went out into the corridor. Sarah had an intense feeling of satisfaction. Not every case had a happy ending, and this could so easily have been otherwise. She adjusted her step to John Simmonds' long strides.

'Coffee, Sarah?' asked the Registrar, as they were going down in the lift.

'I think I should be getting back to the ward,' she

replied, her pulse beginning to race automatically.

'A few minutes won't make much difference,' he said suavely. 'Sister has given you permission, and the ward is quiet this afternoon.'

That's true, thought Sarah. But I don't want to be alone with John Simmonds . . .

'Besides, you've been looking tired this week. You need to take a break. The patients will benefit in the long run, you know.'

Was he mocking her? She watched helplessly as he re-programmed the lift for lower ground floor.

'I've got a room in the residents' quarters, and a jar of instant.'

The lift stopped, and she stepped out, her heart beating wildly. His room was the usual clutter of text-books, case histories and discarded surgical gowns. It would have been impossible to swing the proverbial cat.

'Sit down, Sarah,' he invited, quickly sweeping aside a pile of books from the divan.

She looked around the room; obviously only used for emergencies—nights when it was too late to go home. The only chair in the room held an even larger pile of books, and Sarah found herself wondering if the cleaners ever ventured as far as John Simmonds' chaotic hideaway. She had an unexpected desire to organise the chaos for him, but remained very still and quiet, watching those long, tapering fingers as they performed the simple task of making coffee. For someone who was an expert in the operating theatre he seemed to be decidedly hopeless in a domestic environment.

He handed her a mug of dark brown liquid, and she gasped as she took the first sip.

'I'm sorry—is it too strong?' he asked, with a wry grin. 'I never know how much you're supposed to use.'

'It's drinkable,' she laughed, and at the sound of her laughter he sat down on the divan beside her, smiling his approval.

'That's better, Sarah. You look much younger when you laugh.'

'I'm only twenty-eight,' she countered jokingly.

'I know.' His voice had a breathless quality she hadn't heard before.

When she turned to look at him, she knew he was going to kiss her. She remained motionless as his lips touched hers, gently at first, then more fiercely, passionately, stirring an infinite longing inside her. Unable to control her mounting excitement, she clung to him, willing the moment to last for ever. As she opened her eyes she saw that he was watching her, with a sad expression. She moved away and tried to stand, but her legs had turned to jelly.

John put out his arm to steady her. 'Don't go, Sarah. We've both suffered so much; we need each other now, and love is an excellent therapy.'

'Love?' she repeated questioningly.

He seemed to emerge from a dream. 'Did I say love?' he murmured softly, but the tender expression had gone from his eyes.

'I'd better get back to the ward,' she said quietly.

He was glad she was going; he couldn't think why he had invited her down in the first place. Perhaps he felt sorry for her . . . but her effect on him was far too disconcerting. Much better to avoid meeting her alone. Now, Liz Stuart—that was something different. You knew where you were with Liz . . .

'Yes, you'd better get a move on,' he said brusquely, as he opened the door. 'Goodbye, Sarah; I hope you enjoy the dance tomorrow.' There was a mischievous gleam in his eyes.

'And I hope you enjoy the theatre,' she replied, without thinking.

A concerned look crossed his face. 'How did you know about that?' he asked.

'You forget, Liz is a friend of mine,' she replied.

'And I suppose you tell each other everything . . .'

'Not quite, but she did say you were taking her out tomorrow.'

'Interesting girl;—have you known her long?'

'Since PTS. Now, I really must be going. Goodbye.'

'Goodbye, Sarah.'

Well, that was the end of that, and a good thing too, she told herself, as she hurried back to the ward.

'How's Mrs Tate?' asked Sister, when she appeared.

'She's fine. It's early days yet, but she's going to be treated as an outpatient.'

'Splendid. Now, could you chase up the juniors with their TPRs, and check on the blood pressures.'

Angela Dawson hurried away; there was always so much to organise when you were having a weekend off. She had no doubt that Sarah was perfectly capable of being left in charge, but the girl was bound to be worrying about her mother's operation, and her own move to Orthopaedics.

In actual fact, Sarah was looking forward to her weekend in charge of Nightingale, and had stopped worrying about her mother, who seemed in excellent spirits.

Everything went smoothly on the ward on Saturday, and she found herself looking forward to the dance in the evening. Mrs Gibson had accepted the fact that she was going out, and had even expressed her approval, to Sarah's surprise; Mr Gibson was going to read the children an extra bedtime story.

When she came off duty, Sarah took a shower in the Nurses' Home before changing into her red cotton dress with the full skirt. As she crossed the road to the medics' hostel, she was poignantly reminded of the many evenings she had spent there with Mark. A tiny tear streaked, unbidden, down her cheek, and she hastily brushed it aside. Passing the Black Bull, she could see a crowd of medics and doctors by the bar. At the edge of the circle, Alan Walker was keeping an eye on the door.

'Sarah!' he called, when he saw her. 'I've been watching out for you—what will you have?'

She went into the crowded pub. Over at a corner table she could see Liz, in earnest conversation with John Simmonds. He was looking devastatingly handsome in an immaculate grey lounge suit, which seemed strangely incongruous amid the scruffy jeans and sweaters of the Saturday night revellers. Liz, too, looked stunning in a fabulous cream linen evening suit—it must have cost a bomb, Sarah thought, irrationally, with a twinge of an unpleasant emotion which she recognised as jealousy. And it was not just about the suit, she admitted reluctantly.

'I'll have an orange juice, please, Alan,' she said, as she joined the crowd by the bar.

'You're looking lovely tonight.' He handed her a glass.

'Thank you.' She forced herself to go along with the general air of jollity.

'Sarah!'

She knew, without turning round, that Liz had come over to the bar. 'Why, what a surprise,' she said, turning to look at her friend. Over Liz's head her eyes met those of John Simmonds.

'Enjoying yourself?' he asked mockingly.

'Yes, very much,' she lied.

Liz's eyes were shining with excitement. 'We've got to dash, Sarah. Curtain up in half an hour—I'll tell you all about it on Monday. Goodbye!'

John Simmonds nodded briefly towards Sarah and Alan and followed the attractive Sister outside.

'Now that's an interesting match,' said Alan.

'Why interesting?' She tried to make her voice sound light.

'Well, I wouldn't have thought Liz was John Simmonds' type.'

'Why ever not?' She gave a brittle laugh, to hide her emotion.

'She's too shallow for him—he's a man of hidden depths, I think,' Alan replied.

'Well, perhaps Liz intends to find out what makes him tick,' Sarah muttered quietly.

'I wish somebody would. Another drink?'

'No, thanks—shouldn't we be getting along to this dance?' The smoky atmosphere of the Black Bull was becoming oppressive.

He took her glass and put it down on the bar. 'Let's go,' he said, taking her arm and steering her out of the pub.

The medics' hostel had changed very little in the intervening years. The large common room in which the dance was being held was exactly as Sarah remembered it—the same dark green curtains, shabby but comfortable sofas pushed against the wall, and continual noticeboards running all round the room. The only thing that had changed was the music. It was much louder, and seemed to be of an entirely new generation.

'How long since you were last here, Sarah?' asked Alan, as if reading her thoughts.

'Must be about five years, I suppose,' she replied, thinking to herself that music couldn't change all that much in so short a time—or could it? Or was she just getting older?

Alan insisted they dance every dance; he was a good dancer, and she enjoyed being whisked around the floor. Her eardrums had adapted to the exuberance of decibels, and she was quite content to go on dancing. About midnight, she glanced at her watch.

'Good heavens, Alan! I didn't realise it was so late,' she exclaimed.

'What's the matter—will your carriage turn into a pumpkin at midnight?'

'No, but I've got to drive back to Riversdale.'

'Well, one for the road?'

Sarah shuddered. 'No, thanks!'

'Where's your car?' he asked.

'It's over in the hospital car park, but I can find my own way.'

'I wouldn't hear of it,' he said, taking her arm.

They walked in companionable silence back to the car. Sarah unlocked the door and was about to step in when she felt his arm go round her waist. She stiffened.

'What's the matter?' he asked. 'I'm not going to hurt you.'

As she turned her head to remonstrate, his hungry lips came down on hers. She struggled furiously, but he maintained the relentless pressure for several seconds before releasing her, a triumphant smile on his face.

'There, that wasn't too bad, was it?' he asked, confidently.

'Why do you automatically think you have a right to kiss a girl, if you take her out for the evening?' Sarah cried furiously.

'Oh, don't be so prudish!' he sneered. 'You knew the score as well as I did. It's so long since you were in a man's arms, you've forgotten what it was like.'

She gave his face a resounding slap. 'How dare you!' she snapped.

Alan laughed, and rubbed his cheek. 'Well, the girl's got spirit, I've got to admit that,' he said. 'Look, I'm sorry, Sarah, if you didn't enjoy that; it'll be better next time . . .'

'You've got a nerve!' she began, but he continued as if nothing had happened.

'It'll be better next time, when we've had time to get to know each other.'

'Good night, Alan.' Sarah slammed the car door and revved the engine.

He stood for a moment at the front of the car, preventing her from driving forward, so she switched into reverse gear and set off.

'OK, you win,' he laughed, as she roared away. What a strange girl! he was thinking as he watched the little red car disappear out of the car park. Still, I suppose I should remember she's a widow. Probably got a few hang-ups about that . . . but it shouldn't be too difficult to break down her resistance . . .

Sarah drove along the deserted streets of Bradfield in a furious temper. If this was what a night out did to you, then she was going to stay in for ever!

Of all the conceited . . . ! Thinks all he has to do is crook his little finger and the girls will come running! she fumed.

She was feeling calmer when she reached Riversdale. There was a light on in the kitchen of the farmhouse.

'Dad!' she exclaimed in surprise, when she saw her father sitting by the dying embers. 'You don't usually stay up this late.'

'I was waiting for you to get back,' he admitted sheepishly. 'I promised your mother I would.'

'I'm not a child,' she said gently.

'Maybe not, but there's a lot can happen on the road between here and Bradfield, and it's nice to know you're safe home.'

'How are the children?' she asked.

Mr Gibson's face creased into a loving smile. 'Just champion! Well, I'll be off to bed now. Do you want wakening, lass?'

'Yes, please, Dad. I'm in charge all day tomorrow. Joanna will be moving in here—I've got Anne's room ready for her, and little Christopher can have the spare room.'

'Yes, I saw your mother in there giving it a good dust today. Good night, Sarah.'

'Good night, Dad,' she said, staring into the remains

of the fire. She felt tired and disillusioned. Her first contact with another man had been repulsive. No one could ever replace Mark, she told herself, as she had done so many times. And yet, when she had been close to John yesterday, she had felt a sudden rush of feeling, something which she thought had died with Mark. It didn't make any sense to her, but her natural dislike of John seemed to be turning to something else.

Whatever it was, it had no place in her scheme of things, and anyway, it was obvious John found Liz more attractive than her. Pull yourself together, girl! You're behaving like a lovesick schoolgirl . . . there, I've admitted it . . . lovesick. But I'm not, she tried to convince herself, but found she was losing the battle. She forced herself to think of something else, as she put out the kitchen light and made her way upstairs, but it was a long time before she fell asleep.

She was in the middle of doing the dressings next morning, when both Dr Simmonds and Dr Walker appeared on the ward, with Mr Shaw. The colour rushed to her face as she hastily disposed of her gown and mask and made her way towards them. Mr Shaw was unpredictable in his Sunday morning rounds, and Sarah had hoped he was going to give it a miss this week. He was in one of his churlish moods, and insisted on seeing all his patients, and arguing their treatment at great length with his houseman and Registrar. When he eventually sailed off through the ward doors, declining the customary coffee, they all breathed a sigh of relief.

'He may not need coffee, but I do, Staff,' said the Registrar, making his way to the side-ward.

'So do I,' agreed the houseman.

'I thought you had a salpingectomy on Cavell?' queried John Simmonds, seemingly reluctant to share his coffee break with the houseman.

'She's still in Recovery—I'll go along when I've had my coffee,' Alan Walker insisted firmly.

Sarah put the kettle on and placed two cups on the table.

'I'm afraid I haven't time to join you, gentlemen,' she said lightly. 'I've got to finish the dressings. The coffee jar is over there . . .'

'Nonsense, girl!' John Simmonds barked. 'Take the weight of your legs for a moment.' He put out an arm and placed her in Sister's chair. As his arm encircled her waist for a brief second, she felt a sharp tingling down her spine. She daren't look up; both pairs of eyes were on her, she knew.

'I'll make the coffee,' Alan was saying. 'My God, the old man was in a foul mood, wasn't he? Must have gone out on the town last night and got a hangover. Rather like I've got.'

Sarah looked up in surprise. 'I didn't know you'd drunk too much last night, Alan.'

'Oh, that was after you'd gone,' he said, with a bitter laugh.

John Simmonds looked at the pair curiously. 'Had a good night, did you?'

'Depends what you mean by good,' Alan remarked cryptically.

'Well, we had a splendid evening at the theatre,' said John. 'And I haven't got a hangover.'

Alan was watching his Registrar closely. Pompous prig! he was thinking. I wish he'd go away, then I can get Sarah on my own and apologise. She's decidedly unfriendly this morning, and I can't really blame her.

'Thank you for the coffee.' John stood up.

He's actually going, I hope . . . thought Sarah. As soon as the Registrar disappeared, Alan turned to her.

'About last night—look, I'm terribly sorry . . .'

'Oh, forget it,' she muttered. 'I've got work to do, and I'm sure you have.'

'When shall I see you again, Sarah?'

'I've no idea—I'm moving to Male Orthopaedic

tomorrow.' And with that Sarah hurried back into the ward.

She finished the dressings quickly and efficiently. By lunchtime the ward looked neat and tidy, ready for the afternoon visitors. Sarah felt a warm glow of satisfaction as she gazed round 'her' ward. She saw her future stretching ahead—more responsibility, and then Sister in charge of her own ward . . . Well, why not? And in a few years she would be as experienced as Sister Dawson. That was a thought which somehow didn't appeal to her.

Sunday afternoon seemed never-ending. There was the usual influx of visitors, but from a medical point of view everything was quiet. The calm before the storm, Sarah mused, as she glanced at the long list of admissions for Monday morning. And there it was, in black and white—Joan Gibson; Wertheim's. She wanted to get home as soon as possible, to see if her mother needed her.

By the time Sarah got back to Riversdale Joanna was installed in the farmhouse, and Joan Gibson had packed her bag ready for the morning. It was something of an anti-climax for Sarah, when she was expecting to be fully in demand.

'Sorry, Sarah,' smiled Joanna. 'I think we've made you redundant here! You can concentrate on your nursing career, and we'll see to the domestic arrangements.'

Joanna was trying to be helpful, but Sarah had an irrational feeling of resentment. She was moving further and further away from her family, becoming more and more of a career girl—well, that was what she wanted, wasn't it?

As she lay in her narrow bed that night, staring out at the big round moon shining through her window, just as she had done when she was a child, she felt very muddled. It was all very well to strike out for independence, but what if she found that wasn't what she really wanted? Suppose she couldn't silence her new feelings?

She turned her head away from the moonlight and closed her eyes wearily. In spite of the fact that she was very tired, it was impossible to sleep.

CHAPTER NINE

SARAH felt decidedly bleary-eyed in the morning, but by the time she reached hospital some of the cobwebs had cleared and she was raring to go again. She'd always enjoyed orthopaedic nursing and was actually looking forward to her temporary transfer. Her mother was in good spirits, and quite ready for her admission to hospital. Mr Gibson was going to drive her in later, so everything seemed under control.

She stood for a moment, drinking in the atmosphere of the male orthopaedic ward. It was still quiet and organised, but there was the expectancy of the hurly-burly to follow. Very soon the ward would hum with the noise of physiotherapists urging the patients to move their muscles, occupational therapists teaching new skills to relieve the boredom of long-stay patients, and exuberant porters moving beds to X-Ray or the plaster room. But for the moment, the ward still belonged to the nurses.

'Sarah! Welcome aboard!' Liz stood up from her desk and came to meet her friend by the door. 'Have I got things to tell you!' she whispered, then, raising her voice and remembering the protocol, she added, 'Come and hear the report, Staff Nurse.'

Sarah was introduced to the night staff, and to her new colleague, Staff Nurse Karen Collins.

'Staff Nurse Williams will be with us for about a month,' explained Liz. 'She's on loan from the Women's.'

There was a friendly atmosphere about the way in which they all sat round Sister's desk, listening to the report, and asking questions. The whole thing was much more democratic than Angela Dawson's stiff and starchy attitude.

This is how I would run my own ward, Sarah found herself thinking.

'OK, any more questions? Fine . . . let's get on with the work. The work lists are here on my desk—tick things off as you do them, please. Nurse Williams, may I see you for a minute before you start?'

'Of course, Sister.'

As soon as the other nurses had left the desk, Liz smiled conspiratorially at Sarah.

'I'm letting you in gently till you feel your feet, Sarah. Would you mind doing some blanket baths with Nurse Finch—it'll help you to get to know the patients.'

'That's fine, Liz. I need to get the feel of the ward before you give me anything difficult.'

'Exactly. So here's the list. We'll have a coffee later, and I'll tell you all about Saturday night,' Liz added, lowering her voice.

'Can't wait!' said Sarah, putting on a bright smile. Nurse Finch was waiting for her, so she stood up and hurried away to the first patient.

'Good morning, Mr Long,' she said to the elderly man, after first glancing at the treatment sheet. 'We've come to make you more comfortable. Where's your sponge bag?'

'It's in my locker somewhere,' replied Mr Long, taking a good look at the new staff nurse. 'I haven't seen you before.'

'That's because I've only just arrived on this ward, but don't look so worried—I used to work here a few years ago.'

'You must have been a child a few years ago,' quipped the elderly patient gallantly, enjoying the unexpected attentions of the two young ladies. This was a nice start to the week.

'Let's have this jacket off, shall we, Mr Long—there

you go.' Sarah put the jacket in his locker and took out a clean one. 'How does your bionic hip feel this morning?'

Mr Long smiled. 'It's still a bit painful, but it's worth it if I can get walking around again. Wonderful what these surgeons can do!'

Sarah washed her patient gently, while he talked about his operation for hip replacement.

'Now, pull yourself forward with your canary perch,' she said, adjusting the pulley, before plumping up the pillows. 'There you are . . . you can come back now.'

Mr Long left go of the handle to his pulley and leaned back gratefully. 'By gum, that feels a lot better. Nurse. I'll have a little rest and then I'll do my exercises, before that physiotherapist gets her hands on me!'

They moved on to the next patient, a young man with a fractured femur, sustained in a motor-cycle crash.

'When are they going to take me down off this contraption, Nurse?' he asked irritably.

'As soon as the bone heals,' said Sarah, looking at the conglomeration of weights and pulleys. She glanced at the notes and saw that he was due for X-ray. 'We'll be able to tell you more when we see the new X-rays. Just pull yourself up off the sheet; we're going to change it.'

Several bed-baths later, Sarah was feeling ready for her coffee break, but not for Liz's saga of her night out with John Simmonds. That was the last thing she wanted to hear about. But when she saw Liz beckoning to her from the ward door, she asked the junior to restock the bathing trolley, and made her way down the ward.

'How are you getting on?' Liz asked, as she poured out the coffee.

'Fine; I'm enjoying myself—makes a change from Gynae.'

'I should think it does; they're strange people on the Gynae firm—take John, for instance.'

Why ever not! thought Sarah wryly. I knew it wouldn't

be long before we had to talk about John . . .

'I mean, he's so . . . er . . . so reticent. He just won't discuss his past, will he, Sarah?'

'I'm sure I don't know. You know him better than I do, Liz,' Sarah replied unconcernedly.

'He told me he'd been out to the farm.'

'Oh, that was quite by chance—he's looking for a house in the area.'

'Is he? Perhaps it's the nesting instinct at work,' said Liz.

'I doubt it,' Sarah countered, a little more vehemently than she intended. 'He hates the whole idea of marriage—he told me he would never go through all that again—those were his very words.'

'Yes, but he could be made to change his mind. Men are very pliable creatures, Sarah. Just because he's had one disastrous marriage, it doesn't make him a bachelor for life.' There was a dreamy, faraway look in Liz's eyes as she said this.

The sound of masculine footsteps marching on to the ward brought Liz back to earth.

'That sounds like someone arriving to do a round,' she commented, making for the door.

Sarah followed, and continued with her bathing routine. Out of the corner of her eye she could see the orthopaedic doctors moving up the ward. When they arrived close to Sarah, Liz introduced them.

'This is my new staff nurse, Nurse Williams, Mr Milner.'

The tall, distinguished-looking consultant smiled briefly at Sarah, before continuing on to the next patient. The Registrar and houseman eyed her appraisingly, thinking she would make a welcome addition to Male Orthopaedic.

After lunch Sarah was free all afternoon, so she made her way to the Women's, to see how her mother was getting on. She found her sitting in a chair by her bedside reading *Jane Eyre*. When Sarah arrived, she looked up sheepishly.

'I've always wanted to read this,' she said, 'but I've never found the time, somehow. I think I'm going to enjoy myself in here, being waited on hand and foot.'

Sarah smiled. 'Have you had any tests yet, Mum?'

'Well, a nice young man took some blood away—here he is, now.'

She looked up in dismay, to see Alan Walker approaching. She'd hoped to avoid him.

'Can't keep away, eh, Sarah?' he observed.

'I suppose you haven't been told that this is my mother?' she replied coldly.

'No, and I'm afraid I hadn't made the connection— but wait a minute . . . those beautiful brown eyes! I might have known, Mrs Gibson . . . so that's where Sarah gets it from!'

Mrs Gibson smiled with pleasure. What a charming young man!

'I've come to take down a few more details . . . no, don't go, Sarah,' he said, as Sarah stood up.

'I can't stay if you're here in a medical capacity, Alan. Sister wouldn't like it. I'll come back this evening, Mum, before I go home.'

'All right, dear. Now what do you want to know, Doctor?'

Sarah went over to the Nurses' Home and spent the afternoon watching an old film on television. There was no one else in the common room, and she almost fell asleep. When it was time to go back on duty she felt better for the rest and relaxation.

'Beds and backs with Nurse Moss, Staff Nurse,' Liz said formally, when she arrived.

Sarah went into the sluice; the junior was setting the trolley and she looked up with interest at the new staff nurse. She seems friendly enough, she thought, as they made their way out on to the ward to start the evening routine.

Tim Farrow, the motor-cycle crash, was as fractious as ever. 'Another month, Nurse!' he complained to Sarah. 'They've done another X-ray and the bone still hasn't joined up. You'd think with all this lot on my leg, it would get a move on, wouldn't you?'

Sarah adjusted the Thomas's splint and the Pearson's knee flection piece. The Steinmann's pin was pulling too much; the weights of the skeletal traction seemed excessive. Sarah looked around for Liz.

'Anything I can do, Staff?' asked the orthopaedic houseman, from the other side of the ward. He was partially hidden behind a curtain, so that Sarah hadn't noticed him.

'Yes, please, Doctor. I was wondering if we could reduce some of the weights on this skeletal traction. It seems to be pulling.'

The houseman came across and smiled at Sarah. 'I'm Barry Law,' he said easily. 'Let's take a look . . . mm, you're right, Nurse. I'll remove some of the weight, like this . . . is that better, Tim?'

'Much better, Doc, but it still feels blinking awful. How would you like to spend weeks and weeks tied up like this?'

'I wouldn't Tim; that's why I don't ride a motor-bike.'

'Oh, very funny!' muttered Tim. 'But I tell you what, Doc; that's the last time I ride a bike, as well—I'm saving up for a car,' he added.

'Heaven help us!' said the houseman. 'If you need me again, Staff, I'll be on the ward for the next hour at least.'

'Thanks, Dr Law.'

Sarah continued down the ward, massaging pressure points, applying ointments, and generally making the patients comfortable. By the time she went off duty she was feeling very much at home on the ward.

'Good night, Sarah. See you tomorrow,' called Liz, from her office.

'Good night, Liz,' Sarah called back, wrapping her cape round her. As she stepped out into the corridor she almost collided with a tall dark figure in an immaculate grey suit.

'Dr Simmonds!' she gasped. 'I didn't expect to see you.'

'Obviously,' he said, in a cool voice. 'I was looking for Sister.'

'Why, John, you're early . . . you said nine o'clock.' Liz came hurrying out of the office, looking flushed and excited.

'Couldn't wait, my dear,' he said, with a charming smile. 'Are you ready?'

Sarah hurried away before she heard any more. It certainly looked as if Liz was breaking down his resistance!

Nightingale Ward was in semi-darkness when she arrived. The junior night nurse was pushing the drinks trolley round, and the charge nurse was giving out medicines. She smiled when she saw Sarah.

'Do you want to see your mother? I think she's nearly asleep over there.'

Sarah approached her mother's bed.

'Hello, Sarah,' Mrs Gibson murmured drowsily. 'Isn't it time you were going home?'

'Yes, but I wanted to see how you were getting on, Mum,' replied Sarah gently.

'I'm fine, dear. Don't worry about me—they're looking after me a treat. You run along now—I expect you're tired, if you've done half the work that these angels have done in here.'

Mrs Gibson had closed her eyes again, so Sarah bent over and kissed her, 'Good night, Mum.'

'Good night, dear.'

As Sarah turned to move away she saw Alan Walker

coming towards her down the ward.

'I thought I might find you here,' he said. 'How about a quick one over at the Bull?'

She opened her mouth to decline, but changed her mind—it might dispel some of her weariness. And there wasn't much could happen to her in a crowded pub.

'OK, but only a fruit juice, Alan.'

'I know, you don't have to tell me—you don't drink and drive,' he repeated solemnly.

Sarah laughed as she followed the fair-haired house-man out through the ward doors.

The Black Bull was crowded as usual, as they pushed their way inside.

'There's a table over there by the window, Sarah—I'll get the drinks,' Alan said.

Sarah forced a path through the sea of bodies, in the direction Alan had pointed. He was much taller than she was—she couldn't for the life of her see an empty table . . . ah, yes, there it was. She stopped short. Another couple were just about to sit down there.

'Sarah!' called Liz. 'Come and join us.'

It was too late to pretend she hadn't seen them. She moved the last few yards towards the table. John Simmonds had remained standing, until she arrived. Now he was holding out a chair for her. As he pushed it under the table she got a whiff of his delectable after-shave. He's obviously out to impress Liz, she thought.

'What are you doing here all alone?' asked Liz, pretending to look scandalised.

'I'm over eighteen . . .' Sarah began with a smile, but John Simmonds interrupted her.

'She's not alone, Liz. The boy-friend's in tow, of course. There he is over at the bar.'

'Oh, you mean Alan.' Liz looked back at her friend. 'You're a dark horse, Sarah!'

'There's really nothing . . .' Sarah began.

'Of course not,' Liz said quickly. 'But I'm glad you're

in circulation again, Sarah.'

Alan arrived, with a drink in each hand, just as John was going to the bar. The look of dismay on his face told Sarah he wasn't happy about sharing a table with his boss.

'Hello, Alan,' Liz said pleasantly. 'I'm glad you're taking care of my staff nurse.'

'It's a pleasure. How are things with you and . . . ?' He jerked his head in the direction of the departing Registrar.

'Couldn't be better,' she purred. 'I was going to tell you about Saturday night, Sarah, but I haven't had a chance all day. We went to see the new Pinter play at the Grand. It was a bit highbrow for me, and I didn't really understand it, but afterwards we drove out to the Country Club and had the most fabulous meal . . .'

Liz's voice droned on, extolling the virtues of her latest conquest, until Sarah's eyes searched the crowded bar for signs of the returning paragon. Anything to stem the flow!

'There you are, Liz,' said John, placing her drink on the table. 'You girls been having a cosy chat?'

'And completely ignoring me,' put in Alan. 'When Liz starts, there's no stopping her . . . all about this fabulous bloke who wined and dined her on Saturday!'

John smiled, his cool, aristocratic smile, and Sarah's heart missed a beat. Her toes curled automatically as she looked at the handsome Registrar. Why did it have to be Liz who had unlocked all that charm? It was the first time she had admitted to herself that she was really jealous. But it was too late now to do anything about it. She drained her glass.

'Another drink, Sarah?' asked John, fixing those deep blue eyes on her face.

'No, thanks—I've got to get back.'

'Oh, yes, the family commitments,' he murmured. 'How are the children?'

'They're very well,' she answered awkwardly, anxious to escape the scrutiny of those disturbing eyes. 'I must go.'

'I'll walk you to the car-park, Sarah,' Alan said.

'No; stay and have another drink,' Sarah insisted firmly.

Might as well, thought Alan. She's scared of a repeat performance. I'll have to give her time to recover. 'OK,' he replied nonchalantly. 'Good night, Sarah.'

She forced her way back through the crowd, and breathed a sigh of relief when at last she reached the cool night air. It was an easy drive home under the starlit sky, and, after a brief chat with her father and Joanna, she climbed thankfully into bed. As she closed her eyes, it was John's face that stayed in her mind, keeping her awake until the small hours.

I never thought I could ever feel like this again, she thought. But this time there's nothing I can do about it.

Liz had assigned Sarah to do the dressings next morning. At last she felt she was dealing with the more interesting aspects of orthopaedics. As she was removing the stitches from a meniscectomy patient, the athletic-looking footballer said to her,

'Are you free on Saturday, Nurse?'

'Why?' she asked, continuing to concentrate on her task.

'Because I'll be out by then, and I thought we could get together—maybe go out for a meal.'

'Sorry, Bobby, I'm fully booked on Saturday—keep still till I've finished.'

He gave her a cheery grin. 'Well, another night, then?' he persisted.

'I'm clean out of baby-sitters at the moment,' she replied, enjoying the surprised look on his face.

'I'm sorry, Nurse; I didn't realise . . .' He looked down at her wedding ring. 'Silly of me—I might have known you'd be spoken for—a good-looking girl like you.'

Spoken for she was not, but it was nice to use it as an excuse; it saved a lot of hassle. 'There we are, Bobby, good as new,' she said briskly, placing the surgical scissors back in the kidney dish.

'I hope so, Nurse; I'm dying to get back on the soccer pitch. Just my luck to wreck my knee up.'

'Well, don't overdo it—take it easy to begin with. Are you doing your quadriceps drill, like the physio showed you?'

'Yes—watch, Nurse.'

'Very good, Bobby,' Sarah said admiringly, and moved on to the next patient.

'Good morning, Mike; are you ready to have your stitches out?'

'You bet, Nurse! Can't wait to get out of this place!'

She had finished the dressings by mid-morning, and went to look on Liz's desk at the work lists. The ringing of the ward phone made her break off.

'Hello; Male Orthopaedic.'

'Casualty Sister here. There's been a pit disaster out at Blackthorne—an explosion or something. They're bringing in the casualties now. Accident and Emergency have more than we can handle, so some of them will have to come straight to the ward. How many beds have you?'

She did a rapid calculation. 'Ten empty, but we're admitting for theatre tomorrow.'

'That will be cancelled—this is an emergency, Staff. The porters will be bringing more beds on to the ward.'

The line went dead. Sarah went to find Liz, to explain the situation.

'Take the two juniors and prepare the admission beds,' Liz said calmly. 'Oh dear, no time for that—here they come!'

The first stretcher had arrived at the ward door. A grimy face with wide, staring eyes peeped out from beneath the red blanket. 'Look after this patient, Sarah,' instructed Liz.

Sarah smiled at the frightened patient. 'Any notes?' she asked the porter.

'You must be joking, Staff—it's like Paddy's market down there! Where would you like him?'

'Bed fourteen—I'll help you.'

There was no time to find an admission blanket; another patient was already arriving. Sarah helped the porter ease the man into bed. Blood was oozing through the patient's pit overalls. Without hesitation, she took out her scissors and cut straight up the trouser leg, to reveal a bony protuberance outside the skin.

'Looks like a tib and fib,' observed the young porter knowledgeably.

'You could well be right,' Sarah agreed.

'My chest hurts,' muttered the patient.

Sarah felt gently over his rib cage. Probably fractured ribs . . . Yes, this seemed to be the place. She made him as comfortable as possible before moving on to the next arrival.

'Head injury,' announced the porter, pushing the stretcher.

Sarah looked at the still figure; beneath the dirt and grime there was an unnatural pallor. Someone down in Casualty had inserted an endo-tracheal tube to help the unconscious patient breathe. Sarah felt for his pulse—it was too rapid. She lifted the blanket. Blood was pouring from a wound in his arm.

'Wait there till I've stemmed the flow—Liz, bring me a tourniquet.' This was no time for protocol.

Liz rushed off to the treatment room, while Sarah kept her hand on the radial artery. As she applied the tourniquet, a tall white-coated figure came up beside her.

'What do you want, Dr Simmonds?' Sarah said brusquely. 'Sister is very busy . . .'

'I came to help,' he replied coldly. 'All available doctors have been drafted to Orthopaedics. Let me take a look here . . . That's good—you've stemmed the flow. Get him into bed and I'll see what I can do. We'll need to replace the fluid he's lost—set up an IV, Nurse Williams.'

'Yes, Doctor.' It seemed perfectly natural to be working with him again, and she was too busy to have any feelings other than a desire to treat as many patients as possible.

The ten beds were soon filled, and still the patients kept coming. The theatres had been turned over to the emergency, and soon the most urgent cases were being operated upon. An emergency plaster area was set up in the treatment room, so that fractures could be treated on the spot. The porters brought more beds, and filled every available space. The normal ward routine was forgotten.

'Hey, Staff Nurse; when are we going to get our dinner—I'm starving!' called the irate footballer, as Sarah hurried past his bed.

He can think of his stomach, at a time like this! she thought. But I suppose I'd better do something or we'll have all the regular patients fainting on us.

'Just coming, Bobby,' she said soothingly. The heated food trolley had been standing inside the ward door for nearly half an hour, and no one had plugged it in. 'Didn't you see the trolley, Nurse Finch?' she snapped at the hapless junior who was hovering nearby.

'No, Staff Nurse. I was busy . . .'

'A nurse is never too busy to be observant,' Sarah began, then stopped. She was beginning to sound just like Angela Dawson! 'Take this light diet to Mr Long,' she added in a gentler tone.

Liz emerged from the treatment room. 'Well done,

Sarah—I'm glad you thought about food. I'll come and give you a hand. We'd better put something on one side for the staff—there's no time to go to the dining-room.'

It wasn't long before the patients' relatives started to arrive. They congregated outside the ward doors, distressed and anxious.

'We haven't got room for relatives on the ward,' Liz said brusquely. 'Let them have two minutes, and then they must go.'

'I'll speak to them on their way out,' put in John Simmonds quietly. 'We can't have them going away in a worried state, and I've been round all the new cases.'

'Thanks, John.' Liz gave him a brilliant smile. 'You're such a help.'

A small, grey-haired woman was peering through the ward doors. Sarah opened them. 'Would you like to come in now?'

'Did he have his wallet on him?' demanded the woman, without preamble.

'What name?' Sarah asked gently.

'Frank Briggs,' replied the woman anxiously. 'I know he had his wallet on him this morning when he set off, because he was going to call at the shops on the way home, seeing as how he was on early turn and me being at work, like.'

The head injury, thought Sarah. 'Yes, I've got his wallet here in the desk. It was in his overalls pocket.'

The woman grabbed the wallet unceremoniously. 'Thanks, Nurse. I'll be able to get something for the kids' tea now. Where is he?'

'Bed fifteen, Mrs Briggs.'

The woman scuttled away, and Liz came over to the desk.

'What a cheek! Asking for his wallet, before she's even seen the poor man. He might have been dead for all she knew!' burst out Liz indignantly.

'She probably loves him very much,' Sarah countered

quietly. 'But when you've got mouths to feed, there's not much you can do without money. I know—I've been hard up myself.'

Liz gave a sniff of disapproval as she made her way back to the treatment room.

'I didn't know you were a philosopher,' observed John Simmonds from the other side of the desk.

'Hardly a philosopher,' smiled Sarah. 'Just something I learned in the early days of my marriage—how to survive.'

'And you survived, and the marriage didn't,' he said softly.

'That was hardly my fault,' she retorted, wondering how she could ever have imagined that she was falling in love with such a callous brute—Liz was welcome to him!

'I didn't say it was,' he replied, in a cold voice. The girl is too touchy for words, he thought. All that pent-up emotion waiting to be released! I could never handle that.

They worked non-stop until nine o'clock, by which time the emergency was under control. It hadn't occurred to anyone to go off duty during the day, but now that the night staff were here, Sarah decided she ought to make tracks for home. Joanna would be getting worried—there'd been no time to phone.

'Do you mind if I go, Liz? They'll be wondering where I've got to at home, and I've got to call in and see how Mum is, on Nightingale.'

'You go, Sarah. And thanks for everything,' said Liz.

'I'll come over to the Women's with you, Sarah.' John Simmonds' suggestion was the last thing she had expected. 'I haven't seen my patients all day.'

'Oh, do you have to go, John?' asked Liz peevishly. 'I've nearly finished this report—I thought we could pop over to the Bull . . .'

'Sorry—not tonight, Liz. Duty calls.'

Liz watched him in exasperation, then bent her head over the report.

John and Sarah walked over to the Women's together in silence. Each of them was wrapped in their own different thoughts. Sarah was worrying about her mother, and John was feeling annoyed at the possessive tone Liz was beginning to use . . . he must avoid any sort of commitment, at all costs. He couldn't afford to lose his freedom at this stage . . .

'Did you see my mother this morning?' Sarah asked suddenly.

'Yes; we've started her blood transfusions. Mr Shaw wanted to raise her haemoglobin as soon as possible.' He looked down at the earnest expression on Sarah's face, and admired the strength of character etched upon it. The poor girl has suffered just as I did, he thought. It's left its mark on everything she does.

Sarah caught the look in his eyes and turned away— one minute he was cold and callous, and the next he was full of tenderness. She quickened her pace and went into Nightingale.

The night nurse was sitting at the desk in a pool of subdued light. She stood up when she saw Dr Simmonds and Staff Nurse Williams.

'Good evening, sir; good evening, Staff; can I help you?'

'We've both come to look at Mrs Gibson, Nurse,' replied the Registrar.

'She's on her second pint, sir,' said the night nurse helpfully. 'I'll take you over . . .'

'No, carry on with your own work, Nurse,' he interrupted quietly, as he started off down the ward.

Mrs Gibson smiled when she saw the nice doctor with her daughter. There was a dim light over her bed, so that the nurses could watch the IV.

'Come to say night-night, have you, Sarah?' she asked softly.

'How are you, Mum?' asked Sarah.

'I'm fine, dear.'

She'd say that even if she was dying, thought Sarah wryly. 'Are you comfy?'

The arm fixed to the IV looked anything but comfy. Mrs Gibson smiled at her daughter. 'I'm doing fine, aren't I, Doctor?'

'A model patient, Mrs Gibson,' he said, looking down into the expressively trusting brown eyes. As tough as an ox, this patient—just like her daughter! 'I'm going to take your blood pressure, Mrs Gibson,' he added.

'I can do that for you,' said Sarah quickly.

'Sorry, Nurse; Sister said you weren't to become involved in the case,' he said, in a cool, professional voice.

'I'll be on my way, then.'

'No, wait—I shan't be long. I thought we could have supper together.'

'I'm exhausted . . .' she began.

'All the more reason for you to have a good meal. I know you've hardly had time to eat anything today.'

That was true. She looked up into the handsome face. 'OK, you win.'

'Good. I'll pick you up at the Nurses' Home in a few minutes.' He turned back to his patient, who was smiling at the pair of them.

'Good night, Mum.' Sarah dropped a kiss on her mother's forehead and left the ward.

She changed quickly and sat down in the foyer. Her heart missed a beat, as the swing door opened and Liz came through.

'Sarah! I thought you'd gone,' Liz exclaimed.

'I've been to see Mum.' Sarah stood up and made for the door.

Liz gave her a strange look. 'How is she?'

'Improving. Good night, Liz.' As she hurried out

on to the front steps, she almost collided with
John Simmonds. He put out his arms to prevent her
stumbling.

'Hey, steady on! What's the hurry?'

'Nothing . . . I just wanted to get away.' She accepted
his arm and allowed him to help her into the waiting car.
Silly to feel so guilty. They were only going out for a little
supper together, and he was probably using her to stop
Liz being so possessive with him.

The blue Mercedes purred out through the hospital
gates, and she wallowed in the luxurious comfort of the
interior—rich leather seats, soft carpets. She was trying
to identify the subdued classical music emanating from
the stereo, when he broke in on her thoughts.

'It's rather late, so I've rung through for a table at
Giovanni's. All the English restaurants will be closed by
now.'

Sarah had heard of Giovanni's . . . chic, expensive,
and reputedly of a very high standard.

'Are you hungry?' he asked.

'I am, now that I've got time to think about it.'

'I'm starving, and I shall enjoy the meal all the more
for having a delightful companion with me.' His eyes
were on the road, so she had no way of knowing if he
were sincere or merely making fun of her.

'You could have taken Liz with you,' she countered
lightly.

'I could, but I chose not to.'

The arrogance of the man! He was simply using her to
get back at Liz. 'Will you bring me back to pick up my
car?' she asked in a cool voice.

'Don't worry about minor details,' he snapped irritably. 'I'll arrange something.'

Sarah opened her mouth to retort, but thought better
of it.

The head waiter greeted them effusively. 'Dr
Simmonds! Delighted to see you again, sir.' He

showed them to a secluded table, neatly tucked away in a palm-fronded corner.

Sarah was aware of John's eyes on her throughout the meal, but she tried not to show it, even though her pulses were racing. The food was delicious, from the very first morsel of lasagne verde, through the vitello scallopino al marsala to the profiteroles. As they finished, Sarah sat back in her chair, her eyes shining.

'Thank you, John. I didn't know I was so ravenous!'

'I'm glad you enjoyed it. I thought you were a more deserving case than Liz.' There was laughter in his eyes, but Sarah didn't like the implication.

'I hope you're not feeling sorry for me,' she said tersely.

'Not at all, my dear,' he replied expansively. 'But Liz can go into the Sisters' dining-room, whereas you've got to go home to look after your family.'

'I can take a hint!' Her tone was bantering, but there was a hostile gleam in her eyes as she stood up.

'Don't be so touchy,' he pleaded gently, his hand on her arm.

'I'm very tired. Will you run me back to the hospital car park?'

'I'm going to take you home.' His tone was masterful; she daren't argue. 'You're too tired to drive. I'll stay at my house in Milesdale and pick you up in the morning.'

'So you bought it, then?'

'It was just what I wanted.'

The road to Riversdale was bathed in moonlight. The countryside had never seemed so beautiful, as she lay back in her seat. Her eyelids closed heavily and she fell into a deep sleep, to be awakened some time later by a pleasant sensation on her lips. She raised a hand to her face and opened her eyes. The car was parked outside the farm, and John was looking down at her tenderly, his lips parted. Whether or not he had just kissed her she would never know, but from the look on his face, she guessed he had.

'The Sleeping Beauty awakes,' he murmured, and leaned forward.

'Is that you, Sarah?' came her father's voice from the kitchen door.

'Just coming, Dad!' She scrambled inelegantly out of the car.

John grinned at her affectionately. 'I'll pick you up about seven-thirty.'

Her heart was beating wildly as she reached the house.

'Wasn't that Dr Simmonds?' asked her father. 'You should have invited him in. Where's your car?'

'I left it at the hospital. We've had an emergency and I was tired,' she explained briefly.

'Nice of him to run you home.'

She slept very little, almost longing for the morning to come. When the blue Mercedes glided into the farm-yard, she hurried outside, but his attitude had changed completely. It was perfectly clear to Sarah that last night meant nothing to him. He was simply being a good doctor, taking care of an overworked nurse. Or was he using me to annoy Liz? she wondered. I'll make sure she never hears about it.

CHAPTER TEN

DURING the next two weeks the emergency situation on Male Orthopaedic gradually eased off. A few of the patients had been taken into intensive care, some had been transferred to other wards, while others were lucky enough to have been discharged, to be treated as out-patients. It began to resemble a hospital ward again, rather than a bomb-site. The pungent smell of coal dust and grimy overalls had been replaced by an air of antiseptic cleanliness once more.

On the morning of her mother's operation, Sarah would have liked something to occupy her totally, to keep her mind off things. Liz, intending to be kind to her friend, had given her an easy work list, so that she was finished by coffee time.

'Stop worrying, Sarah,' said Liz, as they drank their coffee together. 'She's got the best surgeon in the business.'

Sarah smiled. 'I suppose you mean John.'

'Who else? He's doing more and more surgery. Mr Shaw's going to miss him, when he gets Mr Thwaite's job.'

'Is it decided?'

'More or less,' Liz replied happily. 'Just imagine . . . I could be a consultant's wife!'

'When's the big day?' Sarah asked lightly.

'Oh, don't be silly, Sarah. He hasn't asked me yet; but I'm working on it . . . Have you really finished your list?' Liz asked, hastily changing the subject.

'Yes, what would you like me to do?'

'You can finish off my dressings for me. Mr Milner and his gang will be here any minute.'

Liz had barely finished speaking when the tall consultant poked his head round the side-ward door.

'Can you spare a minute, Sister?' he asked politely.

Liz got to her feet and went back into the ward, followed quickly by Sarah.

When she went down for lunch, Sarah was surprised to see Julie already at a table in the staff dining-room.

'What's this, then? Since when have the PTS taken to having their meals in the staff dining-room?' asked Sarah, sitting down beside her sister.

'I couldn't concentrate, so Sister said I could come and see you. Have you heard anything yet?' Julie looked anxiously at her sister.

'Not a thing, but then I'm over on Orthopaedics, so I know as little as you do.'

'When can we go and see her?'

'Sister Dawson said this evening would be OK. Mum's way down on the list, and it's a long operation—I don't want to keep pestering them. I'll ring this afternoon, from the ward.'

'What time are you off duty, Sarah?' Julie asked in a small voice.

'Not until six o'clock, so you go back to PTS and get some work done. You can meet me when I come off duty, and we'll go and see Mum together.'

'OK,' agreed Julie reluctantly. 'I suppose I'd better get back.'

'Have you had your lunch?' asked Sarah sharply.

'I've had a little—I wasn't hungry. See you at six.' Julie skipped away quickly, before her sister could insist she eat something else.

Promptly at six o'clock, Julie was waiting outside Male Orthopaedic, hoping Sarah would get off on time for once. As the doors opened, she smiled.

'Come on, Sarah,' said Julie, breathing a sigh of relief. 'Did you phone Nightingale?'

'Yes, but she was still in Recovery—that was a couple

of hours ago. She should be back by now.'

When they reached the ward, Sister Dawson came bustling up to meet them.

'Your mother's still very weak, so don't stay long, Nurse Williams,' she said, completely ignoring Julie.

Sarah went quietly down the ward. It seemed like foreign territory. Strange to think she would be returning here in a couple of weeks. Julie tiptoed behind her, overawed by the intravenous drips, and the tense atmosphere of the ward on theatre day. She barely recognised her mother. The pale, unconscious figure, still in theatre gown, bore no resemblance to the tough matriarch who presided over the farm at Riversdale.

A tear stole down Julie's cheek, and Sarah squeezed her hand.

'She . . . she's all right, isn't she, Sarah?' Julie whispered.

'Yes; she's a good colour,' Sarah said.

Julie looked at the deathly pallor, and wondered what a bad colour would look like.

'What's the drip for?' she asked curiously.

'She's lost a lot of blood—we've got to keep the haemoglobin level up . . .' Sarah paused, as a shadow fell across the bed.

Dr Simmonds had come to see his patient. It had been a long, difficult operation, but he had successfully removed the malignant area. The prognosis was good. He rubbed a hand wearily over his forehead, surprised to find that he was still wearing his theatre cap.

'I'll take that for you, Dr Simmonds,' said Sister, gliding silently up to the bed. 'I've told Nurse Williams she mustn't stay too long.'

'That's all right, Sister. I'd like to speak to her,' John Simmonds said.

'Very well, Doctor.' Sister Dawson moved away down the ward.

'I think we caught it just in time,' he said quietly.

'Another week or two and who knows? It was an invasive carcinoma, but it hadn't spread to the lymphatics.'

'So she stands a good chance of total recovery?' Sarah
asked hopefully.

'Let's not count our chickens, Sarah,' he said briefly.

She noticed the tired lines round his eyes, as he
screwed them up to adjust the IV. His broad shoulders
sagged as he stepped back to write something on the
treatment sheet.

'You look whacked, John,' she told him, suddenly
feeling an overwhelming desire to soothe away the stress
from his tired body.

He looked gently down at her, surprised at the sympathetic tone, and their eyes met for a brief instant.

'I am whacked, Sarah,' he admitted. 'But it's nothing
that a good night's sleep can't cure,' he added briskly.

'We'll leave you to get on, then. Come along, Julie.'
Sarah walked away from the bed as quickly as she could,
not wishing to prolong the encounter.

'Good night, Sister,' she said, as she passed the desk.

'Good night, Nurse Williams.'

The ward doors were barely closed before Julie began
discussing John Simmonds.

'Isn't he gorgeous, Sarah? If I didn't know you better,
I'd say you had a crush on him!'

'Don't be silly, Julie—only schoolgirls have crushes.
He's a very good doctor, and I'm glad he's looking after
Mum,' Sarah said quickly.

'So'm I. I feel better now I've seen her, even though
she did look awful. She's out of danger, isn't she, Sarah?'

'I hope so,' Sarah replied. 'Do you want me to drop
you off at PTS?'

'No, thanks. I've got to go to the Nurses' Home
library. I'll see you tomorrow—and thanks for holding
my hand, big sister,' Julie said, with a wide grin.

''Bye, Julie.' Sarah went over to the car park and
drove out through the hospital gates. She was feeling

much happier than she had done for several days.

Mr Gibson hurried out of the house to meet her.

'How is she, Sarah? They wouldn't tell me anything when I rang up—as well as can be expected—now, what on earth does that mean, for heaven's sake?'

'She's doing very well, Dad; not out of the wood yet, but the operation was a success.'

'Thank God!' breathed her father, with a sigh of relief. 'David's been a bit restless tonight—I think he senses something's wrong.'

'I'll go and have a look at him,' Sarah said, going into the house.

Joanna was knitting by the fire. 'How's your mother, Sarah?' she asked anxiously.

'She's had a successful Wertheim's—well, as far as anyone can tell at this stage. She's not properly round yet. I'm going to look at the children, then I'll go straight to bed,' Sarah answered wearily.

'Don't you want a drink?'

'No, thanks—I just want to sleep. Good night.'

She made her way up the stairs. David's door was wide open.

'Is that you, Mum?' came a hopeful little voice.

Sarah peeped in and crossed to his bed. 'It's time you were asleep, David,' she said gently.

'Why's Grandma gone to hospital?' he asked plaintively.

'There was something wrong inside her body, and the doctors have put it right . . .'

'What's cancer, Mum?'

Sarah took a deep breath; wherever had he heard that? Children took in more than you gave them credit for. 'It's when the cells of the body keep on growing when they shouldn't do.'

David was silent for a few moments. 'And was Grandma like that before she went to hospital?' he asked thoughtfully.

'Yes; she had a few bad cells in her body, but a clever surgeon has taken them away.'

'That was kind of him,' David said, with a smile.

'Yes, wasn't it . . . actually, David, it was that nice man who caught you in the dinghy—do you remember?'

''Course I remember—I like him. He came to see my battleship, and we talked about boats, and the sea, and . . . oh, everything. I think I'd like to be a doctor like him when I'm grown up, Mum.'

'Would you, dear?'

'My daddy was a doctor, wasn't he?'

'Yes, he was,' replied Sarah, with a lump in her throat.

'I wish I still had a daddy, Mum . . .'

'So do I.' Sarah bent down and kissed the fair head on the pillow. 'Good night, David.'

'Good night, Mum. Are you taking us to school in the morning?' he added quietly.

'Sorry—I'm on duty at eight.'

'That's OK . . . ' Joanna will take us,' he said, in his big-boy voice. 'Only Fiona misses you a lot.'

'I'll be home early tomorrow, David,' Sarah offered, in a placating voice.

'Oh, good. That'll be nice for her.' David had already closed his eyes. She felt as if she had been dismissed, as she dropped a kiss on Fiona's forehead and went off to her own bedroom.

As she closed the door, all her determination to be brave collapsed into a flood of tears, and she lay on the narrow bed, sobbing into the pillow. David was growing up without a father, and she was making things worse by spending most of her time at the hospital. Children needed more than material comforts—they needed the love and understanding of a mother and a father. She came to a decision—when Joanna goes to Saudi Arabia in the spring, I'll give up nursing and stay at home, she thought. I can return to hospital when they're grown up. There was nothing she could do about the lack of a father, but she was going to make sure they didn't miss their mother.

The next couple of weeks on Male Orthopaedic passed quickly for Sarah. Every day she went to see her mother, and found herself looking forward to returning to work on Nightingale.

'It won't be long now, Sarah,' said Sister Dawson, with a knowing smile. 'Your mother can go home at the weekend.'

'That's good news, Sister. She's looking well, isn't she?'

'She's a remarkable lady,' pronounced Sister. 'Got a lot of spirit—but you mustn't let her overdo things when she gets home. Have you got any help?'

'Joanna Lindley is staying with us for a while,' Sarah told her.

'Ah, yes; Joanna—a good nurse, as I remember. Married, isn't she?'

'Yes, but her husband's away on a course,' explained Sarah.

'I see—well, between you, I think you'll manage to cope very well.'

When Sarah told her father the good news, he was overjoyed.

'We'll have a little party,' he said, looking as happy as a schoolboy.

'Mum's got to be quiet at first, Dad,' Sarah put in tentatively. 'I think a party might be too much for her.'

'Oh, nothing much, lass—bake a cake or something,' was his vague response.

'I'll make a chocolate cake,' said Joanna quickly. 'Mrs Gibson likes my chocolate cake. Sarah hasn't got time to bake.'

I haven't got time for anything at the moment, Sarah thought ruefully. But I'll make time for Mum's homecoming. She had persuaded Liz to give her a half day on Sunday, her last day on Male Orthopaedic.

Mrs Gibson was sitting up in bed when Sarah got home on Sunday afternoon. Joanna was busy in the kitchen, icing the chocolate cake, and the children had been told to play quietly until teatime. Mr Gibson was busy with the hay in the barn. Work on the farm couldn't stop just because it was Sunday—and a very special Sunday at that.

'How are you feeling now, Mum?' asked Sarah.

'I'm feeling very well, dear. I can't think why Joanna wants me to rest—she's been bossing me around ever since she picked me up this morning. She's worse than Sister Dawson!'

Sarah smiled at the comparison. 'Joanna knows what she's doing, Mum. She is a trained nurse, you know.'

'Go and fetch the children, Sarah, there's a dear,' whispered Mrs Gibson. 'I've hardly seen them since I got home.'

'They're coming up at teatime, Mum,' said Sarah firmly. 'We're all going to have tea in here with you.'

'Rubbish!' Mrs Gibson flung back the covers and eased her feet over the side of the bed. 'What an idea! Tea in the bedroom, indeed! We'll have tea round the kitchen table, just like we always do. You've got to have standards, Sarah.'

She's better, all right! Sarah thought. Let's hope she stays that way.

Mrs Gibson sat in an armchair by the fire until tea was ready. The children, delighted to have their Grandma back in the land of the living, played happily on the rug by her feet. Fiona and David were trying to finish a jigsaw puzzle, but as quickly as they put in a piece, little Christopher removed it.

'You're a pest!' shouted Fiona in exasperation. 'I wish you'd go away!'

Christopher started to cry, and ran over to his mother.

'Don't be mean, Fiona,' said David, in a grown-up voice. 'He's only a little boy. You were a pest when you were his age.'

'I wasn't as bad as him!'

'Yes, you were. Don't worry, Chris—I'll play with you,' said David, going across the kitchen.

'What a good boy you are!' Joanna smiled down at David. He was such a help with the younger children. Sometimes she was afraid he was growing up too quickly. That's what comes of having no father, she thought; he's trying to be the man of the family.

By the time they sat down for tea, the children were friends again. Mrs Gibson complimented Joanna on her chocolate cake, but lamented the lack of home-baked bread.

'I'll show you how to make it this week, Joanna,' she said. 'There's nothing like it—this shop-bought stuff is terrible. You don't know what's in it.'

'I don't think you should be making bread on your first week back, Mum,' Sarah began, but realised she might as well save her breath.

'I know how to take care of myself, Sarah, and I shan't get better on shop-bought bread, I can tell you!'

Sarah glanced across the table at Joanna, and gave her a sympathetic smile. She was not going to have an easy time during the next few weeks.

It was almost a relief to be back in hospital next morning. Sister Dawson greeted her like a long-lost friend.

'Welcome back, Sarah. How's your mother?'

'Fine—there's no holding her. She's planning to bake this morning.'

Angela Dawson smiled. 'Joanna will look after her I'm sure. And now, if you're ready for the report, Nurse . . .'

It was good to be back!

The routine on Nightingale hadn't changed. Monday

was admissions day, Tuesday and Thursday were theatre days; Wednesday and Friday were always busy days, looking after the post-operative patients. Occasionally the weekends were quiet, but more often than not there would be an emergency admission or two. The weeks passed, and often Sarah found that she barely saw the daylight. It was dark when she drove in in the morning, and it was dark when she went back to Riversdale in the evening. The work was interesting and very satisfying, but the prospect of a few days off at Christmas seemed luxurious. The thought of four whole days without having to leave the farm!

It would have been nice to spend Christmas in hospital, if she had had no family commitments. Sarah remembered the hilarious ward parties, with one of the surgeons coming in on Christmas Day to carve the turkey. It had been fun before she was married, but this year she wanted to be with her children—and Angela Dawson had agreed.

'They need you at home, Sarah,' she had said kindly. 'I've got no family, so I don't mind being on duty—I quite enjoy it, actually.' It was true. She enjoyed a Christmas sherry with Mr Thwaite, and he looked so handsome as she stood beside him when he carved the turkey. Yes, hospital was the best place to be at Christmas, if you hadn't got a husband . . .

Two days before Christmas there was a party in the Nurses' Home.

'You've got to come, Sarah,' urged Liz. 'Everybody will be there. And you're going home for four days, so they can't begrudge you a little fun on your own.'

Sarah had agreed, but she didn't relish the thought of watching the flourishing love affair between Liz and John. As she changed out of her uniform, she wondered what on earth had made her say yes. Was it too late to back down now?

'There you are, Sarah.' Liz poked her head round the

changing room door. She was wearing a stunning white cat-suit. 'Do you want to use my room to get dressed in?'

'No, I'm OK here.'

'Well, buck up, then. What are you wearing? Oh, that's sweet.' Liz had picked up the black skirt and blouse she had brought with her. The blouse looked decidedly crumpled from its day in her bag. The outfit had seemed attractive last Christmas, but Sarah wasn't so sure about tonight. She really should have bought something for the occasion—if only she'd had time! And she was saving every penny now that she had decided to stop work in the spring.

Loud pop music was blaring out of the speakers in the common room as Sarah followed Liz through the door. Balloons and streamers hung from the ceiling, and there was a huge Christmas tree over in the corner. Along the far wall, a long trestle table had been set up as a bar. Alan Walker waved to them.

'What will you have, girls? . . . No, don't tell me—let me guess; gin and tonic for Liz, and a fruit juice for Sarah 'cos she's driving!'

'Brilliant memory you have, Alan,' said Liz with a smile, as she accepted her drink. She glanced round the room. 'Have you seen John anywhere?'

'He was still on Nightingale when I left,' Alan replied.

'Oh, really, he's too much! He always keeps me waiting. I'm not surprised his first wife left him—serves him right!'

They sat down at a table, and Sarah took a sip of her drink. 'Has he ever told you what happened, Liz?' she asked thoughtfully.

'Oh, he refuses to discuss it, whenever I broach the subject. It's very strange—I know absolutely nothing about him, but I think they must have had a blazing row, and she walked out on him. Here he comes, at last!' Liz switched on her most charming smile. 'Darling,' she purred, 'we've been here ages.'

'I couldn't get away,' he said curtly. 'I thought you were going to fix the IV on Mrs Lloyd, Alan?'

'Did you?' asked Alan, his eyes widening insolently.

'Yes, I did. In future . . .'

'Oh, John, be quiet!' interrupted Liz impatiently. 'Stop talking shop—we're here to enjoy ourselves. Come and have a dance.'

She dragged the protesting Registrar to his feet again, and led him on to the dancing area. Alan put his glass on the table.

'Come on, Sarah, you heard what Liz said—we're here to enjoy ourselves!'

He took her arm and whirled her on to the dance floor. It was the first time his arm had been round her since that night in the car park, and she was glad she didn't shudder. On the contrary, it was a pleasant feeling to be moving around in a man's arms again. Perhaps she'd misjudged him.

Liz and John seemed to have sorted out their relationship when Sarah and Alan got back to the table. They were laughing at some private joke, which finished as soon as the other two joined them.

'Dance, Liz?' asked Alan, without sitting down.

'What energy!' laughed Liz, as she stood up and took his arm.

Sarah sat down at the table, wishing the other two hadn't gone off and left her alone with John. For a few moments neither of them spoke, but Sarah was aware of those deep blue eyes watching her.

'Would you like to dance, Sarah?' he asked quietly.

'You don't have to ask me, John, just because the other two are dancing,' she replied evenly.

'Dammit, girl, I'd like to dance with you!'

She looked at him, surprised at the urgent tone of his voice. He smiled at her and stood up.

'I didn't mean to snap, Sarah—I'm a bit tired, that's

all.' He held out his hand; as she took it, his fingers closed round hers.

Her pulse raced as they reached the floor. It was so long since she had felt excited like this . . . she shivered as his arm encircled her waist. It was a slow, romantic dance, and Sarah wanted it to go on for ever—anything to prolong the contact with that strong, masculine body . . .

As the music stopped, he released his hold and looked down at her, a strange expression in his eyes. 'Thank you, Sarah,' he said softly.

She didn't trust herself to speak, as they walked back to join the others.

She found herself longing for another dance with him, but he turned his full attention on Liz. He was only being polite, she thought, as she glided away on to the floor with Alan.

There was a buffet supper of cold meats and salads.

'Mm, this is good,' Alan said. 'Did you girls have anything to do with this?'

''Fraid not,' confessed Liz. 'I've been much too busy, haven't I, darling?' she looked up into John's eyes.

'It hasn't all been my fault,' he replied, smiling back at her. 'We've only been out a couple of times this week.'

'And I've always got to get home in the evenings,' added Sarah hastily. 'I rarely join in the social life here.'

'Oh, but in a way I envy you, Sarah,' said Liz. 'Going home to that lovely farm and those delightful children. I'd love to get away from hospital life for a change.'

'You'll have to come home with me some time, Liz . . .'

'I'd like that—remember when we were in PTS, and you invited me home for the weekend, and your father tried to teach me how to milk a cow?'

Both girls shrieked with laughter.

'. . . It was hilarious,' Liz continued. 'And your father was so patient, and I was hopeless!'

'When are you free over Christmas, Liz?' Sarah asked when they had stopped laughing.

'Tomorrow evening—oh, but that's Christmas Eve.'

'That's all right; we always have a special family dinner in the evening.'

'Do you mind if John comes along, too?'

'Not at all,' Sarah replied calmly.

'I wouldn't dream of imposing upon you . . .' John began, but Liz cut him short.

'Oh, don't be so stuffy! They're a very hospitable family. Sarah's mum will be thrilled to see you—didn't you do her op?'

'Well, if you're sure that's all right, Sarah?' he said, ignoring Liz for the moment. 'It would be nice to spend Christmas Eve in a real family.'

As she drove home Sarah began to have her doubts about the following evening. She had never intended to include John in the invitation. It was a spur-of-the moment idea for old times' sake. Still, it looked as if Liz went everywhere with John now. She would just have to grin and bear it.

CHAPTER ELEVEN

MRS GIBSON was delighted next morning when Sarah told her that Liz and Dr Simmonds were coming for dinner.

'How lovely!' she smiled, looking up from the pastry she was rolling out. 'I do like Dr Simmonds, and we haven't seen Liz for ages—they're going out together, then?'

'Yes, they are,' Sarah replied quietly.

'Well, she's a lucky girl,' Mrs Gibson said, continuing with her mince pies. I wish Sarah could meet someone like that, she was thinking. 'Go and get your sisters out of bed, Sarah. They can't lie in bed all day. There's a lot to be done before this evening.'

Sarah went upstairs and tapped on her sister Anne's door.

'Come in,' said a sleepy voice.

Sarah pushed open the door. 'Mum says it's time you came downstairs,' she told the recumbent form.

Anne groaned. 'It's worse than being on duty—she doesn't change, our Mum, does she?'

Sarah smiled. 'Nothing can change Mum. You'd better observe the house rules while you're here, Anne.'

'Can I borrow your shampoo, Sarah?' Anne ran her fingers through the long chestnut-coloured hair on the pillow. 'I haven't had time to wash it while I was travelling.'

'Of course you can, but don't hog the bathroom all morning—Julie hasn't got up yet.'

Julie was out for the count when Sarah went in her bedroom. She shook her sister gently before getting any response.

'It's Christmas Eve,' Julie moaned, 'I don't have to get up on Christmas Eve . . .'

'Oh, yes, you do—Mum wants you in the kitchen.'

When she got back downstairs Sarah found the men sitting at the table, waiting for their breakfast. Mike had been out with his father, to help with the milking. In his farm overalls he looked younger than his twenty-four years. It was difficult to believe he was already a qualified doctor. Mrs Gibson had left her baking to attend to her menfolk.

'Fetch me some more eggs from the pantry,' she ordered, as soon as Sarah arrived.

'I'll go . . .' began Mike, but his mother interrupted.

'Sit down, Michael; Sarah will go.'

Sarah hurried off for the eggs. She knew her place! There was men's work and women's work on the Gibson farm, and you weren't allowed to mix the two.

The children came racing in from the farmyard, kicking off their wellingtons noisily in the porch.

'Can I help, Grandma?' asked Fiona, climbing up on to the high stool that was reserved for budding cooks. Sarah herself had spent many hours rolling out a piece of dough next to her mother, when she was small.

'In a minute, dear,' said Mrs Gibson patiently. 'Let me finish these breakfasts first.'

The excitement mounted as the day wore on, and not just for the children. Sarah found herself looking forward to the evening. She had accepted the fact that Liz and John were a couple; she would simply have to play the role of good hostess. All the same, she spent a long time choosing her dress.

'Wow, that looks super!' Julie cried, as she burst into Sarah's room in the early evening. 'Is that to impress Dr Simmonds?'

'This is to impress everyone,' replied Sarah casually, as she twirled round in front of the long mirror.

'Well, you look really nice, Sis. It's a pity he's spoken for!'

Julie ran out before Sarah could reply. Little sisters are a nuisance, she thought. Always prodding you where it hurts most.

She stared at herself in the mirror. It was traditional in the family to wear a long dress for the Christmas Eve dinner, and Sarah had accumulated several over the years. This one, in red velvet, was her favourite. She'd worn it for her first Christmas with Mark, and then lovingly put it away. The figure was the same, but he wouldn't have approved of my short hair, she thought wryly, as she ran a comb through it.

'Can I come in, Sarah?' said Anne, as she pushed open the door. 'Oh, good! I'm glad you're wearing long—I wondered if we'd caught up with the latest fashions.'

'No chance!' Sarah laughed.

'Just as well, because they haven't got too many boutiques out in darkest Africa. I think I'll wear that green one I wore last Christmas.'

'You look good in that, Anne. It goes well with your hair, and it makes your eyes look greener than usual.'

'I'm not sure if that's a compliment or not, Sarah. Have you any perfume I can borrow—that's another thing you can't get in the tropics. It goes off in the heat.'

'Help yourself—I'll go and see if Mum needs a hand.'

The table in the dining-room had been covered with a starched white linen cloth. Sarah had set the table earlier in the day, with Julie's help, and it looked very attractive. They had used the best silver and the crystal glasses, and placed a Christmas cracker by the side of each plate. Mr Gibson had lit a log fire in the huge stone fireplace, which illuminated the decorations on the Christmas tree. David and Fiona were sitting on the floor beside the tree, gazing in wonder at the mountain of Christmas presents beneath it.

'When can we open our prezzies, Mum?' Fiona asked, just as she always did, already knowing the answer.

'Tomorrow, Fiona,' David put in quickly. 'After breakfast, if you're a good girl.'

Sarah smiled at his big brother voice. 'If you're very good, both of you, I'll let you stay up until our visitors come,' she promised.

'Who's coming, Mum?' David asked.

'My friend Liz and Dr Simmonds.'

'Oh, goody . . . will he play with me?' the little boy asked.

'There won't be much time before dinner,' Sarah told him. 'Have you finished your supper?'

David nodded.

'Well, go and get ready for bed; come down in your dressing gowns—and don't forget your slippers.'

The two children ran upstairs, excited at the prospect of staying up late. By the time Sarah heard a car in the farmyard, they had returned and were sitting on the rug by the fire, looking like a pair of angels. Sarah looked out of the window. John Simmonds was manoeuvring the blue Mercedes as far as the kitchen door, probably out of deference for Liz's shoes.

Mrs Gibson had already opened the door. 'Sorry about the mud, Doctor; we've had that much rain lately. No chance of a white Christmas this year . . . hello, Liz; good to see you; Sarah tells me you're a Ward Sister now, that's nice.'

'These are for you, Mrs Gibson,' said John, handing her a large bouquet of flowers wrapped in expensive paper.

'Why, how beautiful, Dr Simmonds!' Mrs Gibson smiled.

'Do you think you could call me John?' he asked, with a boyish grin.

'Of course, John. Come inside and let me find a vase—I don't know if I've got one big enough. . . .'

'Good evening, Sarah,' John Simmonds said formally. He looked unbelievably handsome in a charcoal grey suit.

Sarah swallowed hard. 'Good evening, John,' she replied, stretching out a hand towards him.

'You're looking lovely, tonight,' he told her.

'Sarah, you should have told me you dress for dinner out here in the country,' Liz admonished her.

Sarah laughed. 'It hadn't occurred to me. It's only a family dinner, but we always dress like this on Christmas Eve. It means you can wear the same dress every year, if you want to. That's a gorgeous suit, Liz.' It was the suit she had worn on her first date with John.

'Thank you.' Liz cast her eyes round the warm kitchen. 'This is just as I remember it, Sarah. It hasn't changed a bit.'

'Come through into the dining-room,' said Sarah, leading the way. 'The children are dying to see you.'

'Hello, David.' John smiled down fondly at the little boy.

'Hello, Dr Simmonds,' David replied gravely. 'It's nice to see you again.'

'It's nice to be here, David. I've brought you a Christmas present, and this is for Fiona . . .'

'Ooh, thank you!' The children tore open their brightly coloured parcels.

'It's a boat!' David pulled the superb model from its box. 'How does it work?'

'It works by remote control; you put it in the water . . .'

Sarah smiled at the happy pair, as they discussed the merits of the magnificent boat, and the possibility of trying it out on the farm pond.

'It's too dark tonight, David,' Sarah said gently.

'Well, tomorrow then, Dr Simmonds?'

'I'm afraid I'll be in hospital all day tomorrow, David.' The little boy's face dropped.

'I'll help you with it, tomorrow,' said his grandpa quickly.

Fiona was playing happily with a beautiful doll. 'What shall I call her, Mummy?' she asked.

'I don't know, dear; you choose a name you like.'

'I'll call her Sarah, 'cos she looks like Mummy before she had her hair cut,' the little girl announced, after a few seconds.

Sarah looked over the top of Fiona's head to where John was watching the children, and their eyes met for a brief moment. Behind the pleasure reflected in his eyes, there was a look of intense sadness.

'It's time the children were in bed, Sarah,' said Mrs Gibson. 'We don't want them to be tired tomorrow.'

Sarah took hold of Fiona's hand.

'Will you take me upstairs, Dr Simmonds?' David asked.

'Only if you'll call me John,' he replied solemnly.

'I'd like to call you John,' David said shyly, holding out his hand.

John hoisted the little boy on to his shoulders and carried him out of the room. Sarah followed with Fiona.

'Look how tall I am, Mummy!' David cried, as they went up the stairs. 'I'm the tallest person in the house!'

They went into the children's bedroom and Sarah pulled back the covers.

'Will you tell me a story, John?' asked David.

'Yes—as soon as you're in bed.'

Both children jumped into their beds and waited expectantly.

'Tell me a story about a boat . . .'

'All right. Once upon a time there was an enormous boat sailing on the sea . . .'

Sarah leaned across to tuck David's covers in, and her hand brushed against John's arm. It was like an electric shock. She took a deep breath to steady her nerves. Seeing him sitting there on David's bed brought a lump to her throat.

'Don't be too long, John,' she whispered. 'Dinner will be ready soon.'

He nodded, without looking up, and continued his story. Sarah glanced back at the rapt expression on the little boy's face before tiptoeing quietly out.

Everyone was gathered in the dining-room when Sarah got downstairs. Mrs Gibson was beginning to worry about her roast beef.

'It'll be overcooked if we don't sit down soon . . .'

'Stop fretting, Mother,' Mr Gibson scolded. 'It's Christmas Eve. Have another sherry.'

'Well, just a small one, Henry.'

The bedtime story was a long one. Sarah glanced at the clock, wondering when John was going to come down. Perhaps he couldn't get away from the children. She went out into the hall. He was coming down the stairs.

'Ah, there you are,' she said brightly. 'I was beginning to think I would have to help you escape.'

He smiled, a long lingering smile. 'I was a willing captive. It was hard to tear myself away.' He was standing very close to her, and she remained motionless, looking up into his deep blue eyes.

'You're under the mistletoe,' he said softly.

The colour rushed to her cheeks, even as he bent swiftly towards her. The touch of his lips on hers sent an ecstatic shiver down her spine. She closed her eyes to savour the moment, but almost immediately he stepped back, and she was left standing there with her eager face uplifted towards his.

'I hope you don't think I . . .' she began, in embarrassment, but he interrupted her quickly.

'Just a little Christmas fun, Sarah; that's all it was.' His eyes showed no emotion, and his mouth was set in a hard line. There was a cold arrogant expression on his face, as he said,

'Shall we go and join the others?'

Sarah felt close to tears as she followed the tall figure into the dining-room. How could he trifle with her emotions like that? But then he didn't know how she felt about him, and she would make sure he never found out.

'At last!' Mrs Gibson said thankfully. 'Sit down, everybody—not you, Julie—you can help me serve.'

The roast beef was perfect, and the Yorkshire pudding which preceded it tasted delicious.

'You're an excellent cook, Mrs Gibson,' John told her with a smile.

'Thank you, John. I'm glad you're enjoying yourself. Would you like a little more?'

'No, thank you.'

'I've made a special pudding.' Mrs Gibson hurried out to the kitchen to fetch the baked Alaska.

'Are you enjoying life in the QA's, Anne?' asked Liz.

'Very much—it's a good way of seeing the world. I've just got back from Africa, and next week I'm going to Hong Kong,' Anne replied.

'It sounds wonderful. I sometimes think I'd like to travel,' Liz began, then paused to look at John. 'I'm afraid I might get homesick,' she added.

'Depends what you have to leave behind at home,' put in Anne, with a knowing look. 'I'm completely free, so I never feel homesick. I'd find it very difficult to settle down in one place.'

Mrs Gibson arrived back with the pudding, which was duly admired by everyone.

'This is good, Mum,' Julie said. 'It's clever the way you get the cold icecream in the middle of the hot meringue. I'd like to try it myself some time.'

'I'll show you how, while you're at home on holiday,' her mother promised.

'How long holiday have you got?' asked Liz.

'A week, and then I go on the wards,' Julie replied importantly.

'Oh, my goodness! We'd better warn the patients,' said Liz. 'Which ward are you going on?'

'Female Medical.'

'That's just down the corridor from me—I'll be able to keep an eye on you,' Liz said, with a smile.

'And how about you, Mike?' asked John. 'How long are you staying in this part of the world?'

'I go back to London on Boxing Day. I was lucky to get Christmas off.'

'You were indeed. When I was a houseman I had to work over Christmas.'

'Yes, but it's not all work,' Liz said. 'Christmas Day is good fun in hospital. We'll have a lovely day tomorrow, as long as there are no emergencies.' She was smiling up into John's eyes.

Sarah got up from the table. 'I'll go and get the coffee, Mum,' she said, as she went quickly out.

As midnight approached, Liz announced that they would have to be going.

'Aren't you going to see Christmas Day in with us?' asked Mrs Gibson.

'No, we really must be getting back,' Liz replied. 'It's been a lovely evening, Mrs Gibson. Thank you so much.'

'It was a pleasure, Liz. You must come again soon.'

'I'd love to.'

'Sarah could bring you home one evening, in the New Year . . .'

Will they never go! Sarah was thinking. Sarah wanted to be alone with her family. It had been a mistake having Liz and John here together. She smiled politely, standing on the step, until John started the blue Mercedes, then she went inside, closing the door firmly behind her. For a moment she leant against it with her eyes shut.

'Tired, Sis?' Mike had come quietly into the kitchen.

'Why, yes . . . it's been a busy week,' she said quickly.

He gave her a shrewd look. 'He's a nice guy, John Simmonds,' he commented.

'Yes, he's just right for Liz,' Sarah said brightly.

'Perhaps,' her brother murmured. 'Come and join the party. The witching hour is nearly upon us.'

The grandfather clock began to strike midnight as they went through into the dining-room.

'Happy Christmas, everybody!'

CHAPTER TWELVE

SARAH found it no hardship to return to hospital after Christmas. She loved the work on Nightingale Ward, and found herself more and more torn between her loyalty to her family and her duty to the patients. The ward was busy with operations on her first day back. She glanced quickly down the list, and went in search of the first patient for pre-med. The treatment sheet said, June Daley, age 28, Laparoscopy, investigation of infertility.

The bed was empty. Sarah looked round the ward.

'Has anyone seen Mrs Daley?' she asked.

'She went off to the bathroom, Staff Nurse,' replied one of the patients helpfully.

Sarah made her way to the end of the ward. 'Mrs Daley?' she called, going out into the bathroom area.

Four patients grouped outside the sluice were engaged in earnest conversation. One of them jumped guiltily, and stubbed her cigarette down the nearest sink.

'Yes, I'm Mrs Daley,' she said quickly. 'It's not time to go down, is it, Nurse?'

'No, but it's time for your pre-med, so you'd better come back to bed.' Sarah said briskly, deciding this was no time to talk about the no-smoking rule. The poor patient looked decidedly nervous.

'I'm absolutely petrified, Nurse,' she confessed, as if to confirm Sarah's suspicions.

'No need to be,' Sarah said with a smile. 'A laparoscopy is a simple operation. You'll be able to go home later today.'

'Yes, but how will they find out what's wrong with me, Nurse?' Mrs Daley asked anxiously.

'Yes, can you explain it to all of us?' said one of

160

the other patients. 'That's what we were just talking about.'

Sarah looked at June Daley's anxious face. 'Do you want me to explain it to everyone?'

'Oh yes, please, Nurse; we're all girls together, aren't we?'

The others laughed.

'Well, I presume you've been married for some time, Mrs Daley,' Sarah began, wishing she'd had time to read the notes.

'Five years, Nurse—and call me June, please. The Mrs bit makes me feel old.'

'Five years, June; and you wanted a baby all the time?' Sarah asked.

'Yes, and they tested my husband and he's all right, so it must be me,' June ended miserably.

'This morning they're going to check if your Fallopian tubes are working properly, by injecting a special dye through them,' Sarah explained. 'They can also have a good look at the ovaries and the general condition of the pelvis.'

'You know, Nurse, I'm desperate to have a baby. I've even considered advertising for one of those surrogate mothers like they have in America. I saw this programme on TV . . .'

'Look no further, dear,' said another patient. 'Having babies is like shelling peas for me. I've had four in six years, and they just keep coming. I can't afford any more, but if we could come to some arrangement . . .'

'My husband has a good job. He'd be willing to pay if . . .'

'Ladies!' Sarah decided it was high time she ended this dangerous discussion. 'I think we ought to find out the results of June's tests before she considers any further action.'

'Yes, but isn't life funny, Nurse?' said the large lady with the four children. 'I mean, here's me with more kids than I can handle, and desperate for a way to stop having any more.'

'Have you tried the pill?'

'Can't take it—I've got high blood pressure.'

'Or the coil?' Sarah continued patiently.

'Don't fancy that at all. A friend of mine . . .'

'What about the sheath?'

'Don't talk to me about the sheath!' the patient groaned, with a derisive shrug of the shoulders.

'The cap?'

'No!'

'Have you thought about sterilisation?' Sarah had come to the end of her ideas, and decided that she must remove her pre-med patient as soon as possible.

'I've thought about it, but that's about as far as I've gone. You see, Nurse, deep down inside me . . .' Her voice trailed away in dismay. She was looking over Sarah's head.

Sarah turned quickly to catch the look of anger on Dr Simmonds' face.

'I wasn't aware that you had opened a consulting room out here, Nurse Williams,' he said coldly.

'I'm simply answering a few of the patients' questions,' she replied evenly, aware of the high colour of her cheeks.

'I would think this is neither the time nor the place, Nurse,' he snapped.

The patients had vanished quickly back into the ward, and Sarah was left alone to face the irate Registrar.

'If a patient asks me a question, I answer it to the best of my ability,' she said, with a calmness she didn't feel.

'You are trained as a nurse,' he cut in, with icy precision. 'Kindly leave the counselling to the doctors, who are better qualified than you to deal with these matters.'

'I don't know how much of this conversation you heard, Dr Simmonds, but I felt it my duty . . .'

'On this occasion you exceeded your duty, Nurse Williams,' he interrupted severely. 'Mrs Daley is one of my patients, and I came to ask her some final questions before I operate. I had hoped to be able to do this on the ward, not in the bathroom area,' he finished pointedly. 'Now, if you wouldn't mind assisting at my examination . . .'

Sarah swallowed hard. It was no good trying to argue with John Simmonds. He wouldn't understand the workings of the female mind. He was too cold and clinical—a brilliant surgeon, yes, but he seemed to be able to dispense with emotions. She began to wonder if, beneath that cold exterior, a real flesh and blood heart was beating. She swept past him angrily, not trusting herself to speak again, but by the time she had reached Mrs Daley's bed, she had recovered her composure. He was only a man, after all. What did he know of the suffering that women had to endure? He might be a doctor, but he had never experienced the agony of a childless woman, nor the weariness of a woman with too many children. She swished the curtains round the bed, venting some of her frustration in the action.

'Good morning, Mrs Daley.' John Simmonds gave the patient the benefit of his most charming smile. 'I'm going to ask you a few questions, before Nurse Williams gives you the pre-med.' He sat down on the counterpane, and June Daley melted visibly in the presence of the handsome Registrar.

Sarah stood quietly to one side, coming forward to assist only when it was absolutely necessary. He had told her to stick to her nursing duties, and that was what she intended to do, from now on!

'Thank you, Nurse,' he said, in his professional voice, when the examination was completed. He turned to go, and Sarah picked up the kidney dish and extricated the syringe. As she gave the injection, she heard him rustle the curtain on his way out, and she gave a sigh of relief.

'I'm sorry if you got into trouble, Nurse,' June Daley apologised. 'You were being so helpful.'

'That's all right, June,' she said, with a smile. 'Now just lie quietly here and rest, until it's time to go down. Don't get out of bed again, because the pre-med will make you drowsy.'

She went out into the ward and crossed to the treatment room, relieved to see that John Simmonds had gone. She plunged the kidney dish viciously into the steriliser, taking comfort from the hot steam on her face. She wanted to purge herself of all feeling for the exacting Registrar.

'Nurse Williams, if you could spare a moment?'

'Yes, Sister.' Sarah gathered her senses together as Sister Dawson came into the treatment room.

'Here is the list of dressings, Perhaps you could start with removal of stitches from Mrs Rogers. She may be able to go home this afternoon, in which case I'd like you to phone her husband.'

Sarah pushed the dressings trolley out into the ward. Mrs Rogers had been an excellent post-operative patient. It was always a pleasure to help her.

'Stitches out today, Mrs Rogers,' Sarah said briskly, as she reached the bedside.

'Marvellous—I can't wait!' Mrs Rogers was already pulling back the covers.

Sarah pulled the curtains round the bed, and went to scrub up at the ward sink.

'Sarah! I was hoping you'd be back on duty. How was your Christmas at home?' Alan Walker had breezed in through the swing doors and was standing beside her.

She shook the water from her hands, and pulled down her mask. 'It was great, Alan. Look, I can't stop now; I'm removing sutures . . .'

'What time are you off?' he asked.

'Six o'clock.'

'Meet me in the Bull—I'll take you out for a meal.'

Sarah paused, aware that Sister was watching them from her desk. Oh, why not? She could ring home. Joanna had moved back into the farm.

'I'd love to,' she smiled.

'Good girl! See you later,' he said, with a dashing smile.

Sarah moved off down the ward, back to the waiting patient, and picked up the sterile forceps. It was a straight clean wound, and Sarah removed the stitches quickly and efficiently.

'There you are, Mrs Rogers . . . as good as new!'

'Thank you, Nurse; now will I be able to go home this afternoon?'

'I don't see why not. I'm just going to ring your husband.'

'Ask him to bring my brown coat—the one with the fur collar—he'll know the one you mean. It looks very cold out there, Nurse.' Mrs Rogers looked out of the window at the frosty covering on the hospital roof and shivered.

'It's freezing,' Sarah agreed. She hadn't enjoyed her drive in that morning. It had been, literally, like skating on an ice rink.

She went to the treatment room to re-set the trolley in preparation for the next patient, before she broke off to make the phone call. Mr Rogers was delighted that his wife was coming home and promised to bring the brown coat. Yes, he knew the one she meant.

The day passed in a flurry of theatre patients, coming and going. June Rogers was quickly round from her laparoscopy, sitting up in bed, demanding to know the results of the infertility tests. Sarah scanned through the report.

'As far as we can tell at this stage, there seems no reason why you can't conceive. There is no blockage in the Fallopian tubes. They've taken a sample from the endometrium for testing. You can go home as soon as the effects of the anaesthetic have worn off.'

'I feel fine, Nurse—and I'm dying for a cigarette and a cup of tea!'

'I'll get you a cup of tea,' said Sarah, with a smile, 'but you can't have a cigarette in here. Anyway, if you're hoping to start a family, you could start practising the no-smoking rule now. Cigarettes and pregnancy don't mix.'

'You really think I could get pregnant, Nurse?' asked June Rogers, her eyes shining with excitement.

'There's no clinical reason why not, but you'd better ask the doctor next week when you come back for your Outpatients appointment.' Sarah went to the kitchen to find a cup of tea. When she returned, June was already dressed and sitting in a chair by her bed.

'Can't wait to leave us, June,' quipped Sarah, handing over the tea.

'Can't wait to get home, you mean,' the patient replied, with a shy grin.

'Just enjoy it, dear,' called Mrs Wilcox, the mother of four, from the next bed. 'Relax and stop worrying, and you'll be surrounded by the little perishers before you know where you are! But just in case you don't strike it lucky, you could always give me a ring.'

Sarah hurried away; she was not going to get involved this time. Let June Daley discuss the problem with a doctor in Outpatients. She found herself wishing it would be John Simmonds. That would teach him to be so high and mighty!

The ward was fairly quiet when she went off duty. The day cases had gone home, and the other theatre patients were fully round, and had been washed and made comfortable. Sarah collected her cape from the side-ward and went off down the chilly corridor out into the frosty night air. The warmth of the Nurses' Home foyer thawed out her hands and feet, as she hurried through to the changing room.

Thank goodness I'm wearing my new skirt, she thought, remembering the early morning fumble for the nearest available clothing at the farm. It was quite by chance that the cream and beige skirt and sweater had been chosen. This was an outfit she had allowed herself to buy for Christmas—expensive, but very good for the morale. She dressed carefully, cleaned her face, and applied new make-up. There, that looked better. What a good thing Joanna was in when she phoned. She seemed positively delighted that Sarah was going out. She was always trying to matchmake.

The Bull was crowded with the six o'clock drinkers, on their way home from the office or the hospital. Alan was already installed by the bar, with her fruit juice ready for her.

'Do you mind going in a foursome, Sarah?' he asked, as soon as she arrived.

'Not at all,' she said, feeling positively relieved. 'Who are the other two?'

'Liz and John,' he replied casually.

'How nice,' Sarah said, maintaining the bright smile on her face with great difficulty. 'I didn't know John was a friend of yours.'

'He's not—purely professional, but I was talking to Liz at lunchtime, and she asked if they could come along.'

'Why not?' she said lightly. 'Liz and I are great friends.' She couldn't help wondering why Liz had invited herself along. Surely a romantic twosome would have been preferable, with the unpredictable Registrar?

The handsome couple walked in through the pub doorway and came over to the bar. They exchanged the usual greetings before deciding where they were going to eat.

'There's a good Chinese in Queen Street,' Liz said.

'I prefer Indian,' Alan ventured.

'What's wrong with English food?' asked Sarah.

'We could always stay here and have a bar snack,' Alan put in, draining his pint and preparing for another one.

'No, let's get away from this area,' said John. 'I know a good restaurant out at Milesdale.'

'You don't mean the Connoisseur, do you?' Sarah asked. 'That's terribly expensive . . .'

'This will be my treat,' he said firmly.

'Oh, but we couldn't possibly . . .' began Alan, meaning exactly the opposite.

'Of course you could,' rejoined John. 'I've already booked the table.'

'So why the discussion?' asked Liz, in surprise.

'Just a little amusement, my dear,' he murmured blandly. 'Let's go, shall we?'

'Wait a minute,' said Sarah. 'The Connoisseur is only two miles from home—I may as well take my car.'

'That's what I thought,' replied John promptly. 'Alan can go with you, and we'll drive him back after the meal. He's already had a couple of pints. Another drink or two will put him over the top for driving.'

'That's very thoughtful of you, John,' said Alan.

The Registrar gave him a withering look, but did not reply.

They drove out of the hospital car park together, Sarah keeping a respectful distance between her little red car and the blue Mercedes. When they arrived at the restaurant she pulled in alongside and switched off the engine. Alan got out of the car and ran round to open her door.

'An impressive place,' he said, as his eyes swept over the illuminated shrubs and trees that surrounded the ornate doorway. 'I bet it costs the earth.'

'It does,' whispered Sarah. 'You might as well enjoy it, if the boss is paying!'

'I intend to,' Alan grinned.

The deferential waiter showed them to a table covered

with a starched white linen cloth. There was a crystal
bowl of Christmas roses in the centre, and the silver
cutlery sparkled in the candlelight. Sarah perused the
enormous menu, and got lost among the starters on the
first page. Alan, too, seemed to be struggling.

'Why don't I order for all of us?' John suggested. 'I
know the dishes they cook best here.'

They all readily agreed, and were delighted with his
selection. The Dover sole was perfect, and seemed to
melt away in the mouth. Sarah looked up from her dish
as John broke the appreciative silence.

'I've got something to tell you,' he began mysteriously. 'I thought this would be as good a time as any to
announce it.'

Nobody moved or spoke. Liz had put down her fork
and was watching John with bated breath. Sarah found
difficulty in breathing. Well, it had only been a matter of
time before he popped the question . . .

'Mr Thwaite will be retiring at Easter, and I've been
appointed consultant in his place.'

You could have heard a pin drop. Liz's face showed
her disappointment. She had known about the appointment from the hospital grapevine, and had hoped it
might nudge him into action.

'Congratulations, darling,' she said, leaning over to
kiss his cheek.

Only Sarah could see the frustration behind the
gesture.

'Well done, John,' Alan said. He raised his glass.
'Here's to the new consultant!'

The duck à l'orange arrived, and Sarah noticed how
little Liz ate. She was simply toying with her food to be
polite, and when the sweet trolley arrived she declined,
saying she had to watch her figure.

Liz and Sarah excused themselves at the coffee stage
and went upstairs to the powder room. As they sat in
front of the luxurious mirror, Sarah said,

'Isn't it good news about John's appointment?'

Liz shrugged despondently. 'I've known about it since before Christmas. I thought he was going to say something else tonight, Sarah.'

'So did I,' said Sarah.

'Did you?' Liz's eyes were wide, as she looked at her friend. 'You know, Sarah, I don't know him any better than the first day we went out together. I sometimes wonder if he's still married, or if he's simply carrying a torch for someone. Whatever it is I'm not waiting around to find out. He's not the only fish in the sea . . .'

'Do you love him, Liz?' Sarah asked softly.

'Good Lord, no! Don't be so romantic, Sarah. I don't think I've ever been in love—not like you and Mark were. I'd like to get married and have children, but I never seem to meet the right person.'

'Give it time, Liz,' Sarah advised. 'And make sure you're in love before you marry. Believe me, it's worth waiting for.'

Liz took her friend's arm. 'Come on, let's join the others, shall we?' she said, with a smile of amusement. What an incurable romantic Sarah was!

John had paid the bill when they returned, and was waiting to leave.

'I've got an early start tomorrow,' he said briskly, holding Liz's fur jacket for her.

'Where shall we drop you, Alan?' Liz asked.

'Somewhere near the residents' quarters,' he replied vaguely. 'I don't want to spoil your evening.'

'You won't spoil our evening,' Liz said pointedly. 'I expect John wants an early night. Why don't you come up for a nightcap, Alan?'

'Thanks, Liz; I'd like that,' he said, surprised at her attentiveness. Well, if Sarah was going straight home, it would make a pleasant end to the evening . . .

Sarah got into her car in the car park and wound down

the window. 'Good night, everybody—and thank you, John, for a super dinner.'

'Good night, Sarah,' they called from the other car. She let in the clutch and drove out through the impressive gateway.

As she arrived back at the frosty farmyard, she couldn't help wondering what her friend was up to—was she trying to play one man off against the other?

CHAPTER THIRTEEN

THE journey from Riversdale to Bradfield got progressively worse in the new year. During January the roads were icy and dangerous in the early mornings, before the gritting lorries had been out, and by the middle of February everywhere was covered with snow.

'You'll have to take a room in the Nurses' Home,' suggested Sister Dawson one morning, when Sarah arrived late on duty. 'Until the bad weather's over, I mean.'

'I can't leave the children, Sister,' Sarah replied, close to tears. She was cold and exhausted from the early morning battle with the elements.

'Yes, but you can't go on like this,' said Angela Dawson kindly. 'Just look at you—worn out before you start! Go and have a hot drink in the side-ward. I can't have you fainting on me!'

Sarah went into the side-ward and closed the door. It was true, she would have to stay in Bradfield until the snow melted. She would get home somehow tonight, and make arrangements with Joanna. But this was the final straw! It wasn't fair on the children. She would give in her notice.

When they're grown up and don't need me, I'll return to nursing, she thought, as she sipped the soothing coffee. She was so wrapped up in her thoughts that she didn't see the grey, distinguished head appear round the doorway.

'Is Sister on the ward, Nurse Williams?'

'Oh, Mr Thwaite! I hadn't seen you.' Sarah put her cup down and started to stand up.

'Don't go, Nurse,' he said, coming quickly into the

172

room and closing the door behind him. 'I'm dying for a coffee, but if Angela sees me she'll start rolling out the red carpet.' His eyes twinkled mischievously.

'Here you are, sir,' she said, handing him a cup.

'You look a bit down in the dumps, Nurse—everything all right?' he asked concernedly.

A tear stole down her cheek, and he reached across to dab it with the immaculate handkerchief from his breast pocket.

'Why don't you tell me all about it, Sarah . . . it is Sarah, isn't it?'

She nodded. 'You must think me such a baby . . . it's just that everything is getting too much. I want to go on nursing—I love it, but I love my children too, and it's impossible to divide myself into two. I think I'm going to have to give up nursing until the children are older.'

'I think that might be a wise decision,' he said gently. 'They're only young once, after all. We shall miss you here—I know Sister thinks the world of you—but it looks as if you ought to put your children first.'

'I'll give in my notice.' Sarah swallowed hard.

'We shall be leaving around the same time,' Mr Thwaite told her. 'I shall be sorry to go, too, but I believe in making way for a younger man. John Simmonds has the brilliance and expertise to make a first-class consultant. I've got no qualms there. Do you find him easy to work with?'

She gave a bitter laugh. 'I think he's an excellent doctor, but he can be very exacting.'

'That's how it should be—I was like that when I was younger, but I've mellowed with age.' He smiled at her. 'Don't be too critical of him, Sarah. He's not had an easy life.'

She looked at him questioningly, but he didn't enlighten her. Plucking up all her courage, she had opened her mouth to ask the question which was uppermost in her mind, when the door burst open.

'Mr Thwaite, what must you think of me?' began Sister, crinkling her eyes engagingly. 'I had no idea you were here . . .'

'That's quite all right, Sister. Nurse Williams has been looking after me. I'd like to do a round of my patients now.' He stood up and made towards the door.

'Another coffee, Vincent?' Sister asked hopefully, but the consultant was hell bent on making his escape.

'No, thank you, Sister,' he said, pausing in the doorway to look round at Sarah. 'Take care of yourself, Nurse Williams.'

She smiled up at him. 'I will—thank you for advising me, sir.'

'I wasn't aware I had,' he said, in a calm voice, and followed Sister into the ward.

Oh, yes, you have, Sarah thought gratefully. The way seems clearer now—I know exactly what I have to do.

Joanna was waiting up for her when she arrived home that night. The house was strangely quiet, with the silence of another snowfall.

'Tired?' asked Joanna, as she handed her a cup of hot cocoa.

Sarah stared into the flames, waiting for the heat to thaw out her fingers. 'I'm exhausted,' she sighed.

'It's this wretched weather, Sarah. It's enough to get anyone down.'

'It's not just the weather, Joanna, although that doesn't help. I've come to the decision that I'll have to give up nursing, until the children are older. I'm missing too much of their childhood.'

Joanna didn't reply at first, but when she did, she looked relieved.

'That makes things easier for me, Sarah. I didn't know how I was going to tell you, but Brian wants us to join him in Saudi Arabia as soon as possible. I got a letter this morning; he's found a house for us, and there's a nice social life out there. I think he's missing us.'

'You must go, Joanna. I knew you would have to leave the farm some time.'

'I'm going out at Easter. That will give me time to wind things up here. There's a lot of arranging to do about the house,' Joanna replied.

'Easter will be a good time for me, too. I'll give in my notice, soon. Meanwhile, I'll pray for good weather,' Sarah added with a wry grin. 'If the snow gets worse tomorrow, I'll have to stay on in the Nurses' Home.'

'You'd better pack a bag, just in case, although the forecast was for a thaw.'

'Let's keep our fingers crossed.' Sarah stood up. 'Will you see to the fire and everything? I'll go and throw some things into a suitcase. Good night.'

'Good night,' replied Joanna, as she busied herself around the kitchen. It was a good thing Sarah had decided to give up work—she didn't feel guilty now at leaving her. She was happy at the prospect of joining her husband. Life was unfair . . . she had so much, and Sarah had so little . . .

Next morning, Sarah was relieved to see that the snow was beginning to melt. I'll take my case with me, but with any luck I should be able to get home tonight again, she thought happily. Sure enough the thaw continued throughout the day. The snowploughs had cleared away the sludge that remained by the time she came off duty.

'Hi, Sis!' called Julie, leaning out of her window in the Nurses' Home. 'Do you want to come up for a coffee?'

'Just a quickie,' Sarah replied, as she ran up the front steps. She took the lift to the second floor and went along the long corridor to Julie's room.

'My goodness, it's just like your room at home!' she said with a laugh, as she looked round at the clutter of clothes and books. Every inch of wall was covered with posters, and the floor was littered with cushions. 'I bet Home Sister loves this!'

'She's instructed the cleaners not to do my room until I

tidy it up.' Julie looked pleased with herself. 'But I don't mind. I prefer it as it is—I'm not going to change it.'

Sarah shook her head. 'And how's your work on Female Medical?'

'Not bad,' replied Julie cautiously. 'I don't think Sister likes me very much—I mean, she's always nagging, but I expect I'll survive. You did,' she finished defiantly.

'I hope you stick it out,' Sarah said. She herself had loved nursing from the very first day. It might not be the right profession for Julie.

'Here's your coffee, Sarah. What's it like out at Riversdale in the snow?'

'It's been dreadful, but it looks as if it's clearing up now. I almost had to move in to the Nurses' Home.'

'Oh, that would have been nice. I wish you had . . .'

'I don't like leaving the children,' Sarah put in quietly.

'No, I suppose not.'

'I went to see Matron, today, to give in my notice,' she went on. 'I've decided to give up nursing.'

Julie's face dropped. 'That's a shame! Is it because of David and Fiona?'

Sarah nodded. 'I'll go back to nursing when they're older.'

'I'll miss you,' Julie told her.

'I'll see you at home. . . . and talking of home, I'd better get a move on.' Sarah jumped to her feet and opened the door. 'Goodbye; be a good girl,' she added, grinning mischievously.

The road to Riversdale was completely clear. There were still some high drifts of snow at the side of the road, but she drove home without difficulty. As she went through the village her eye caught sight of a distinctive blue car outside the village store. She slowed down automatically. It couldn't be . . . yes, it was! The tall, distinguished-looking owner of the blue Mercedes was emerging from the shop, carrying a huge can of paint. The thick woollen sweater changed his appearance somewhat, and the paint-stained jeans bore no resemblance to the well-cut suits he wore in hospital. He could hardly avoid noticing Sarah, as she stared through the car window. Embarrassed at her curiosity, Sarah was about to move on, but he flagged her down.

'Tell your father I've got the paint I want,' he said, smiling boyishly through the open window. 'I met him on the road from Milesdale, and he told me I might get some here. Oh, and tell him I've bought a ladder, so I shan't need to borrow his . . .'

His hand on the car door prevented her from moving off. It was strange to see the surgeon's long, sensitive hands, covered in paint. She shivered as she looked up into those deep, penetrating eyes.

'I'm sorry, Sarah; you must be cold, with the window down. Why don't you come to the house for a cup of tea? I've just lit a fire. Follow me down the road—it's not far.'

He assumed she would follow him, as he got into his own car. She drove after him dutifully, wondering why he only had to crook his little finger and she willingly obeyed.

The house was set well back from the road, at the end of a long private drive. It was a delightful place, stone-built and spacious—more of a family house than a bachelor pad, Sarah thought to herself, as he ushered her through the door. Perhaps the mysterious Mrs Simmonds was about to return to her errant husband?

'Come into the sitting-room,' he was saying, as he opened a huge door to reveal oak beams and an inglenook fireplace. 'This is the only habitable room at the moment, apart from one of the bedrooms.'

'Why, it's beautiful!' she breathed, as she sank down on to the thick carpet in the front of the fire, spreading her hands towards the flames.

John smiled at the spontaneous, childlike gesture. 'I'll get the tea,' he told her.

When he returned, Sarah was as warm as toast. There was a friendly feeling about the house. She felt as if she'd known it all her life. It's the sort of house you could bring up a family in, she thought wistfully.

John sat down on the carpet beside her. There was a faraway look in his eyes as he turned towards her.

'Your hair looks beautiful in the firelight,' he murmured. 'All soft and shiny.' He reached forward and ran his fingers gently through it.

She shivered.

'Not still cold?'

'No,' she whispered happily, as she slipped easily into his waiting arms.

He pulled her gently down until they were lying side by side in the warm glow of the firelight. Softly he kissed her, and her body melted against his. She could feel the hard contours of his virile body pulsating against her. As his sensitive fingers began to caress her, gently at first and then with a demanding urgency, she wanted to abandon herself to him completely.

Suddenly his caresses ceased abruptly; he pulled himself away, panting breathlessly. 'No, Sarah; not like this,' he muttered softly, almost to himself.

Sarah sat up, smoothing back her ruffled hair as she waited nervously until he spoke again. When he did, his voice seemed normal again.

'You're my first visitor,' he said, as he spread himself in one of the fireside chairs.

'Really?' Sarah was surprised.

'I intended not to show the house to anyone until it was absolutely finished, but meeting you in the village just now . . .' His voice trailed away.

'So it was an impulsive gesture,' she supplied, in a cool voice.

'Something like that. I thought it would be nice to get a female reaction to the place.'

Female reaction indeed! she thought angrily. Well,

he's had all the reaction he's getting from me. I've simply
made a fool of myself again. Tears welled into her eyes
as blindly she stumbled to her feet.

'I've got to go,' she muttered hurriedly.

'Sarah, wait!'

'I'll see myself out.'

He didn't try to stop her. She knew he was watching
from the window as she let out the clutch and pressed
hard on the accelerator. Silly of me to get the wrong
idea! she thought. He only wanted to sound me out
about the place. He's obviously getting it ready for
someone . . .

Sarah heard no more about the house at Milesdale and
she didn't mention it to her colleagues in hospital. It had
nothing to do with her, and she would soon be leaving
Nightingale. Better not stir up gossip about the new
consultant, although it certainly looked as if he was
planning to settle down.

The snow and slush of February gave way to the
blustery March winds, and then there was a touch of
spring in the air. As Easter approached, Sarah began to
notice the first flowers in the fields. There were prim-
roses in the kitchen garden, and wild daffodils down by
the river. After Easter she would have time to take the
children on a picnic again. Her thoughts flew back to that
autumn day when John had saved David, in the dinghy.
It seemed so long ago, now.

The new consultant seemed to be avoiding her, or
perhaps it was just that he came on the ward less
frequently now. Whatever the reason, Sarah rarely saw
John Simmonds, and she forced herself not to think
about him.

At the beginning of her last week on Nightingale, a
couple of ex-patients called in on their way from Outpatients. This often happened, but Sarah was particu-
larly delighted to see Samantha Brown down the ward,

carrying a tiny slumbering baby wrapped in a woolly shawl.

'Samantha!' Sarah cried in delight, forgetting all her training as she ran down the ward to gaze at the little bundle.

'Isn't she lovely, Nurse?' Samantha said proudly. 'My Jim's over the moon!'

'And wait till you hear my news, Staff!' June Daley began, hardly able to contain herself with excitement.

Sarah glanced at the happy face and smiled. 'I couldn't begin to guess, June. You'll have to tell me.'

'I'm pregnant!'

'No—I don't believe it!' Sarah feigned surprise. 'Well, aren't you the clever one?'

'It was my operation,' June said, with conviction. 'I just went home and said to myself, there's nothing wrong with me, so I'm going to relax—and it worked! I saw that new consultant, today—Dr Simmonds—didn't he use to be on this ward, Nurse? You know, the one with the blue eyes and sexy smile.'

Sarah nodded, amused at the description.

'Been promoted, has he?' June Daley asked, then continued, without waiting for an answer, 'I'm not surprised.'

As she drove home that evening Sarah felt sad at the prospect of leaving nursing. It was days like this that made it all worth while. Less than a week to go . . .

CHAPTER FOURTEEN

It was Angela Dawson who persuaded Sarah to go to the Easter Dance. She had decided it was just what the girl needed to put some life back into her.

'Everybody will be going, my dear,' she said, as they finished spring-cleaning the linen cupboard. 'And you won't get a chance to go dancing when you're down on the farm all the time.'

She means well, thought Sarah, but I wish she'd stop trying to mother me. Liz had already asked her to go to the dance, and she hadn't made up her mind.

'I've got some tickets to sell,' Sister persisted. 'All the proceeds go to charity.'

'Very well, Sister; you talked me into it,' Sarah sighed, with a resigned smile. She could buy a ticket to keep everybody quiet; she didn't have to actually go.

But two days later, as she was getting ready to leave the house, she decided to pack one of her dresses. The red taffeta with the full skirt and petticoat would be suitable.

'Do you mind if I'm late home tonight, Joanna?' she asked. 'It's the Easter Dance in the Nurses' Home.'

Joanna's smiling face showed her approval. 'Be as late as you like,' she said. 'And enjoy yourself!'

Sarah waved her hand to Joanna as she drove out through the farm gates. She's still hoping I'll find the man of my dreams before she goes to Saudi Arabia . . . Some chance! she thought.

Every minute on the ward was precious to Sarah. She was constantly being reminded that she had only two days left . . . and she wasn't ready to leave. She didn't want to bury herself away in the country.

Liz called in at the end of the afternoon. 'Well, have you decided yet?' she asked.

'Yes, I'm going,' Sarah replied, in a small voice.

'Good girl—how long before you're off duty?'

'Another hour.'

'Come up to my room—you can change there.'

Angela Dawson had given herself a half day in which to get ready. She was hoping for a dance with Vincent Thwaite. It might be the last time she saw him, now that he had retired.

Staff Nurse Fielding was left in charge when Sarah went off duty. 'I feel like Cinderella,' she said, with a wry smile. 'But I *shall* go to the ball when the night staff come on. See you later!'

There was an air of excitement as Sarah stepped into the Nurses' Home foyer. Everyone was busily bustling around in preparation for the great event. Home Sister went past, carrying a tray of savouries.

'Coming to the dance, Sarah?' she called, in a friendly voice.

'Of course; I wouldn't miss it for anything!'

Sarah ran lightly up the stairs to the first floor and knocked on Liz's door.

'Come in—oh, Sarah, thank goodness you're here! What do you think of this dress I bought?' Liz twirled round, in a dove-grey chiffon creation.

'It looks very good, Liz. I'm going to have a shower.'

'Borrow my things, if you need them.'

When the two friends went down to the hall, they caused quite a stir. Alan Walker made a beeline across the dance floor, followed by Barry Law, the orthopaedic houseman.

'We've come to ask the most beautiful girls in the room to dance,' Alan said gallantly. He held his hand out to Liz, and she whirled away with him.

Sarah smiled shyly at Barry; she had got to know him briefly when she was on Orthopaedics.

'May I have this dance, Sarah?' he said formally.

It was an old-fashioned foxtrot and he muffed his steps several times. As he trod on her toe for the second time, he grinned and said,

'Sorry; I'm not much of a dancer—I didn't know we were going to have to do these archaic steps.'

Sarah laughed. 'Matron insists we keep the old dances going. It's all very well for her—she probably learned the steps at school.'

'Shall we sit this one out?'

'Oh, yes, please!'

The young houseman smiled at her alacrity. 'Let me get you a drink to compensate for my lack of expertise.'

'I'd like an orange juice, please.' Sarah watched him skirting his way round the crowded dance floor. She could see many familiar faces. There was Vincent Thwaite, resplendent in a dark suit, with bow tie, turning around the room with Angela Dawson; he saw Sarah over the top of his partner's head and gave her a broad, conspiratorial wink. The look of utter bliss on Sister Dawson's face said it all.

Sarah smiled across the room at the helpful consultant. She was going to miss him. Most of the other consultants were there, she noticed. In fact, Julie had been quite right when she said the dance would be mostly for senior staff—well, she hadn't put it like that.

'I'm not going to a dance with a load of old fogeys!' had been her choice of phrase, Sarah remembered.

She couldn't see the new gynaecological consultant . . . Probably still getting his love-nest ready . . .

'Oh, thank you, Barry.' Sarah took her glass and set it on the table.

The dance finished, and they were joined by Alan and Liz.

'Chicken!' exclaimed Alan, as they sat down. 'At least I made an attempt at it.'

'And I've got the bruises to prove it,' said Liz amiably.

'I shan't dance with you again for a while,' Alan retorted. 'Sarah, will you do me the honour . . . oh, that's better.'

The music was indeed a well-known hit, and they moved easily around the floor. Matron, Sarah noticed, was sitting this one out.

As the evening wore on, everyone became more relaxed and happy. Sarah began to look at her watch during the last half hour, wondering whether she should try to escape out of the car park before the final rush.

'Nonsense!' said Alan. 'You can't go yet. Have another drink. Fruit juice, is it?'

She nodded, thinking, I'll just drink this and then I'll slip away . . . And then she saw him.

He looked tired as he came into the crowded room and crossed to Matron's table to make his apologies. He was still wearing the same suit he had had on earlier in the day, when he did a ward round on Nightingale. She could see Matron nodding her approval at what he was saying. There had obviously been some kind of an emergency, which had detained him in hospital.

Sarah took a deep breath—somehow she had lost her desire to leave. It was unlikely that he would even notice her, but still, it would be nice to watch him, for the last time. There were only two more days to leaving hospital, and John Simmonds didn't do a ward round on those days.

He had asked Matron to dance. Sarah saw them moving nearer towards her across the floor.

'Ready for another drink, Sarah?' Alan was swaying unsteadily in front of her.

She knocked back her fruit juice and handed him the empty glass. Anything to make him move out of the way. John Simmonds was only yards away from her now . . . and then he noticed her. He smiled over the top of Matron's head, and Sarah's heart gave a lurch. Those liquid blue eyes held hers, as if by magic. She couldn't turn away.

Alan returned, and she sipped more fruit juice, but still she watched that tall, fascinating figure. It was the last dance. Alan and Liz were already moving away. Barry stood up to ask her.

'No, thank you,' she heard herself saying. 'I may have to leave early.'

He was coming across the floor—he couldn't be coming for her—but he was looking straight into her eyes.

'May I have the last dance with you, Sarah?' he said solemnly.

Her legs trembled as she stood up and melted into his arms. He held her close to his strong, masculine body, and as they moved slowly in time to the haunting, romantic music, Sarah felt as if she were dreaming. Any minute now she would wake up . . . He relaxed his arms and looked down at her tenderly.

'You're looking very beautiful tonight, Sarah,' he said gently.

She didn't trust herself to speak. Just go on holding me like this for ever, she was praying. The music stopped and the harsh neon lights went on. The band were playing the National Anthem. Sarah was desperately aware of John's taut, rigid body standing to attention by her side.

'May I run you home?' he asked softly, as the band finished.

Everyone was hurrying around, looking for coats and handbags, sorting out lifts, and who was going in whose car.

'Coming up for a coffee?' Liz asked simultaneously.

'I'm going home, Liz—I've got my car, John,' Sarah began, trying desperately to deal with her confused emotions.

'You could leave it here,' he suggested.

'I've got to get back in the morning. I'm on duty at

eight . . .' She was merely thinking out loud, trying to see a way round the problem, but the tender look in his eyes vanished.

'Then I won't detain you,' he said coldly. 'Good night, Sarah.'

He was walking away from her, back across the room to a crowd of doctors. She wanted to scream after him, Come back! But she'd had her chance, and she'd thrown it away. Blindly she hurried from the room and out to the car park. She didn't want to collect her things from Liz's room, and risk their enquiring remarks.

She started the engine and manoeuvred the car through the gates out on to the main road, and was soon going down the long hill on the outskirts of the town. Halfway down, she reduced her speed. The traffic lights were at green, but even so, Sarah always slowed down as she went through them.

It all happened so quickly. Sarah slammed on her brakes as a car crossed in front of her, like a bat out of hell. The young driver had completely ignored the red lights against him. There was an almight thud, and Sarah's car came to rest, embedded in the wreckage of the other one. The seat-belt was painful against her chest, but it had saved her life. She climbed out through her shattered windscreen, wincing at the pain in her chest—probably cracked a rib, she thought.

Several people were gathering at the roadside, shouting to her.

'Stand back—it's going to blow up!'

She looked at the other car, smouldering ominously; there were two people inside the wreckage. The young driver was moaning quietly, still strapped in his seat.

Sarah leaned through the broken window. 'Can you move? We've got to get you out of here.'

The young man looked at her vacantly, then as if coming to his senses, he undid his seat-belt and staggered out.

'Stand back!' the onlookers were screaming. 'Get away from the car!'

'My girl-friend's still in there!' cried the young man.

Sarah could see the inert form, slumped unconscious in the passenger seat. Sarah didn't know whether she was alive or dead, but she had to save her. One of the men from the roadside had dragged the hysterical driver away from the scene and was giving him first aid. There was only Sarah left at the wreckage. She reached into the car, feeling for the clasp of the seat-belt. As she released it, she dragged the young girl out through the shattered window, and fell backwards, with the dead weight on top of her. She was aware of arms pulling the two of them away from the car, and then there was a horrific noise as the car exploded; she saw the flames shooting up towards the dark sky, before she blacked out . . .

When she came to, she could smell the comforting, aseptic smell of the hospital. There was a tall figure bending over her. Through the mists of consciousness she tried to make out who he was.

'Thank God!' he breathed, as she opened her eyes. 'They told me you had head and chest injuries. I expected to find you in Intensive Care.'

Sarah gave a wan smile. 'What happened, John?'

'Hush, darling . . . later.'

Faint as she was, she noticed the use of the word darling. She looked steadily into the expressive blue eyes and saw no hint of sadness.

'It was exactly like the last time,' he murmured, almost to himself. 'I'd seen that idiot Alan Walker plying you with drink . . .'

'Would you believe I was drinking orange juice?' she asked.

'I believe anything you tell me,' he said lovingly, then broke off, as Casualty Sister came into the cubicle. 'How are the young couple, Sister?'

'They'll live,' she said grimly. 'The girl was badly burned on her legs. Do you think she would have had a better chance if she hadn't been strapped in, sir?'

'Absolutely not! It was the seat-belts that saved their lives—without them they would have gone through the windscreen. Sarah survived and was able to save the others.'

Sarah looked puzzled. 'Ah, now I remember . . .' she began, but John gently silenced her.

'Sister, do you think we could have a few minutes alone? There's something I have to tell Sarah . . .'

Sister gave them a knowing smile as she went out into the casualty department.

Sarah waited expectantly; John had taken hold of her hand, and the feel of his fingers was unnerving her.

'As I said, it was exactly like last time.' He paused, and drew in his breath. 'My wife was in a car crash, but she didn't survive—nor did my baby daughter.' He tightened the grip on Sarah's hand.

'I'm so terribly sorry, John,' she said gently. 'I had no idea . . .'

It sounded trite and unfeeling to her own ears, but what could she say? All the time she had known him, she had thought him harsh and cold, when in fact he had been suffering from a broken heart.

'Do you want to tell me about it?' she asked softly.

He nodded gratefully. For five years he had been unable to speak of that fatal day when he had lost his loved ones, but now, at last . . .

'We were living in Somerset—I was a partner in my father's country practice. I had no ambitions in those days; I never thought I would return to hospital. I was booked to open the village fête, but there was a crash on the motorway and I was called away. Jane said she would do it for me, and she took Sally with her. Afterwards she was invited back to the vicarage; the vicar and his wife

offered her a sherry, Jane didn't drink—she accepted
one to be polite. She felt relieved that it had all gone
well, and she allowed them to top up her glass several
times.'

He took a deep breath to steady his voice. Sarah could
see that he was reliving that fateful day.

'On the way home, a car came out of a side road
without stopping, and Jane and Sally were killed.'

Tears had sprung into Sarah's eyes.

'I'm sorry, darling; I shouldn't be upsetting you at a
time like this—but I've wanted to tell you, for so long. In
a way I felt it was my fault . . .'

'No; you were not to blame,' Sarah told him, reaching
up to touch his face.

John bent towards her and brushed his lips lightly
across her cheek.

'They did a blood test on Jane, and she was over the
legal limit—she didn't even like alcohol. That was the
ironic thing. The press went to town—you should have
seen the headlines!—Local Doctor's Wife Drinks and
Drives . . . And all this at a time when I was filled with
grief! In the end, I decided to move away and make a
new life for myself. As soon as my father had found
another partner, I took this job in Bradfield.'

He gazed tenderly down at her.

'I never thought I could go through all that again, but
tonight, as I waited for you to come round, I knew that if
this was the price you have to pay for loving someone . . .'

He broke off, looking into her eyes for some response.

'I do love you, Sarah. I always have—ever since the
first moment I saw you. I've fought against it, but it's no
use. Will you marry me?'

She held out her arms in reply, and he buried his face
in her neck. 'When they said you had head and chest
injuries . . .'

'You're the one who needs the intensive care,' put in

Sarah shyly. 'And I think I'm the one who can give it to you.'

'You mean a sort of love therapy?' he asked gently.

'Love therapy, intensive care, call it what you like,' she answered, with a mischievous smile. 'But I think the patient will require a lifetime's treatment.'

'Then the answer's yes, Sarah?'

'Yes, yes, yes!' She began to laugh with joy, but stopped quickly. 'Ouch, that hurts!' she exclaimed, putting a hand to her chest.

'I think you've got a fractured rib,' said John, reaching his hand to touch the injured place.

Their eyes met, and Sarah smiled. 'Are you treating me in a professional capacity, Doctor?'

His arms closed round her and his lips came down softly on hers. She forgot her discomfort in the ecstasy of that all-consuming embrace.

'I'll treat you in every way possible,' he murmured. 'Just as soon as I get you home.'

'Home?' she queried.

'Our home, Sarah. All the time I was getting it ready, I found myself thinking of you. I didn't know if I dare commit myself again, and I didn't want to hurt you. But that day, when I took you to the house, I knew beyond the shadow of a doubt that we were made for each other. I wanted to propose, but I felt it was too soon for you, that you weren't ready to love again, so I let you go . . . but I've never stopped loving you, wanting you . . .'

'And I simply wanted to place myself in your hands, darling,' she told him happily. 'In your healing hands— because whenever I'm with you, I feel like a whole person again. But I thought you were in love with Liz.'

'Never!' he laughed. 'She was simply an amusing companion, that's all. There was no commitment there, whereas you moved me so profoundly . . .'

He broke off to kiss her again, gently, lovingly, his eyes full of tenderness. 'We'll be together for ever,' he whispered. 'Helping each other through whatever the future holds. We'll fill the house full of children . . .'

'Steady on! I've only got two . . .' protested Sarah.

'There's plenty of time—we've got a whole lifetime, together.'

'They're ready for Staff Nurse Williams in X-Ray, sir,' Sister called, through the curtains.

'Thank you, Sister; she'll be ready in a moment.'

Doctor Nurse Romances

WHAT A GAS!

It's

BILL HOEST'S

uproarious new collection

EVEN MORE BUMPER SNICKERS

It's time to hit the road again with EVEN MORE BUMPER SNICKERS, the third volume in the zany cartoon series that steers you down the humor highway and packs so many chuckles to the mile that you'll never stop smiling.

More Hilarious Humor from SIGNET

- ☐ **AGATHA CRUMM by Bill Hoest.** (W9422—$1.50)
- ☐ **THE LOCKHORNS—"IS THIS THE STEAK OR THE CHAR-COAL?" by Bill Hoest.** (Y8475—$1.25)
- ☐ **THE LOCKHORNS #6—"OF COURSE I LOVE YOU—WHAT DO I KNOW?" by Bill Hoest.** (E9984—$1.75)
- ☐ **THE LOCKHORNS #2—"LORETTA, THE MEATLOAF IS MOVING" by Bill Hoest.** (Y8167—$1.25)
- ☐ **THE LOCKHORNS #5—"I SEE YOU BURNED THE COLD CUTS AGAIN" by Bill Hoest.** (W9711—$1.50)
- ☐ **THIS BOOK IS FOR THE BIRDS by Tom Wilson.** (Y9080—$1.25)
- ☐ **IT'S HARD TO BE HIP OVER THIRTY by Judith Viorst.** (Y4124—$1.25)
- ☐ **PEOPLE AND OTHER AGGRAVATIONS by Judith Viorst.** (Y5016—$1.25)
- ☐ **MIXED NUTS by E.C. McKenzie.** (Y8091—$1.25)
- ☐ **SALTED PEANUTS by E.C. McKenzie.** (Y9547—$1.25)
- ☐ **MORE BUMPER SNICKERS by Bill Hoest.** (W8762—$1.50)

EVEN MORE BUMPER SNICKERS

By
Bill Hoest

A SIGNET BOOK

NEW AMERICAN LIBRARY

TIMES MIRROR

NAL BOOKS ARE AVAILABLE AT QUANTITY DIS-
COUNTS WHEN USED TO PROMOTE PRODUCTS OR
SERVICES. FOR INFORMATION PLEASE WRITE TO
PREMIUM MARKETING DIVISION, THE NEW AMER-
ICAN LIBRARY, INC., 1633 BROADWAY, NEW YORK,
NEW YORK 10019.

Copyright © 1979, 1980, 1981, 1982 by Wm. Hoest Enterprises, Inc.

SIGNET TRADEMARK REG. U.S. PAT. OFF. AND FOREIGN COUNTRIES
REGISTERED TRADEMARK—MARCA REGISTRADA
HECHO EN CHICAGO, U.S.A.

SIGNET, SIGNET CLASSICS, MENTOR, PLUME, MERIDIAN AND
NAL BOOKS are published by The New American Library, Inc.,
1633 Broadway, New York, New York 10019

First Printing, February, 1982

1 2 3 4 5 6 7 8 9

PRINTED IN THE UNITED STATES OF AMERICA

EVEN MORE
BUMPER
SNICKERS

"WELL, IF YOU ASK ME, THIS IS NOT THE NEW
ENGLAND THRUWAY."

"TAKE MY ADVICE . . . PARK IT IN YOUR FRONT YARD, PAINT IT WHITE AND PLANT GERANIUMS IN IT."

WATCH
THIS
SPACE

"SINCE WHEN ARE DOORS 'OPTIONAL EQUIPMENT'?"

"I COULDN'T MAKE UP MY MIND!"

"THAT FIVE DOLLARS? THAT'S FOR WRITING THE BILL."

"DON'T JUST SIT THERE, MURRAY. CRAWL
UNDER AND PUT A DIME IN THE METER."

"IT'S NOTHING FANCY, BUT IT GETS ME THERE AND GETS ME BACK."

"WASHING THE CAR?"

"YOU'RE GOING TOO FAST . . . WATCH THAT BUMP, RING YOUR BELL!"

"WOW! A HUNDRED AND EIGHTY-FIVE! WE'RE
REALLY MOVIN'!"

"LOOK . . . WHO'S DRIVING THIS CAR—YOU OR YOUR MOTHER?"

"WELL, HURRY, MARTHA . . . CAN WE OR CAN'T WE?"

19

"SURE . . . WHAT KIND OF FAVOR?"

"DAMN IT, LADY, YOU CAN'T PLEAD
TEMPORARY INSANITY FOR OVERTIME
PARKING."

"BUT I COULDN'T HAVE BEEN GOING 70 MILES
AN HOUR! I ONLY LEFT HOME TWENTY
MINUTES AGO."

WATCH OUT . . . HERE COMES ANOTHER ONE!"

"DID YOU WARN HIM ABOUT THE BRAKES?"

"FOR HEAVEN'S SAKE, SYLVIA! WHOSE SIDE ARE YOU ON?"

"THAT WAS VERY GOOD, HELEN EXCEPT FOR ONE THING . . . WE'RE IN MURRAY LENHART'S GARAGE!"

"JOGGER? WHAT JOGGER?"

"WELL, IF YOU SELL USED CARS YOU SHOULD EXPECT GUILT FEELINGS!"

"THE SCHNEIDERS HAVE A GARAGE, THE
WHEATLEYS HAVE A GARAGE, THE SLOKUMS
HAVE A GARAGE . . ."

"BE CAREFUL LOUISE. LAST TIME YOU HAD A CUP OF COFFEE WITH SOMEONE YOU WOUND UP IN ALBUQUERQUE!"

"I'D SAY DETROIT HAS CUT 'EM DOWN ABOUT AS FAR AS THEY CAN GO!"

"HI YA, MURRAY! HOW DID YOUR DIVORCE
TURN OUT?"

"DID IT EVER OCCUR TO YOU THAT YOU JUST
MAY BE A LOUSY TEACHER?"

"THIS PART HERE IS THE BRAKE."

"HE'S ONLY SIX. I GET BETTER PICKUP WITH AN EIGHT."

"OF COURSE HE'S PROUD . . . HE'S THE ONLY USED CAR SALESMAN UP HERE."

"MY HUSBAND WILL BE FURIOUS . . . HE JUST
CHANGED THE OIL."

"THIS WAY, DUMMY! WE'RE APPEALING A SPEEDING TICKET, REMEMBER?"

"SEPARATE CHECKS, PLEASE."

"NOW THERE'S A FELLOW WHO'S GETTING OFF ON THE RIGHT FOOT "

"WELL, YOU FINALLY GOT YOUR CONVERTIBLE, MURRAY!"

"NO, I'M NOT SURE IT NEEDS A NEW CARBURETOR. IT'S JUST THAT I'M ESPECIALLY GOOD AT REPLACING CARBURETORS!"

"WELL, WELL . . . IF IT ISN'T THE AUTO MECHANIC WHO CHARGED ME $300 FOR A TUNE-UP"

"...PLUS TAX!"

"... ALTERNATE SIDE OF THE STREET PARKING
REGULATIONS HAVE BEEN SUSPENDED ..."

"WHAT DO YOU MEAN WE'VE RUN OUT
OF AIR?"

"AND TELL YOUR MOTHER TO STOP YELLING
'WHIPLASH' EVERY TIME I STOP FOR A
RED LIGHT!"

"CUT THAT TURN PRETTY CLOSE, DIDN'T YOU?"

"OH DEAR, I HOPE A SPEEDING TICKET WON'T HURT MY HUSBAND'S CHANCES FOR REELECTION AS MAYOR!"

"IF GOD HAD MEANT US TO FLY WE'D HAVE
BEEN BORN NEARER TO THE AIRPORTS!"

"OH, NO, SIR. THAT'S JUST FOR THE
WINDSHIELD . . . THE CAR IS EXTRA."

"MAYBE I SHOULDN'T COMPLAIN, BUT THESE
ITALIAN ALPS LOOK JUST LIKE THE SWISS ALPS
WE SAW YESTERDAY."

"THIS IS DR. GETTINGER. MY CAR WAS ACTING
UP TODAY AND I WANTED TO TALK TO YOU
ABOUT IT."

"IF YOU INSIST ON REARRANGING THE FURNITURE, WHY DON'T I JUST SLAM ON THE BRAKES?"

"WE OUGHT TO HAVE A GOOD HOT BATH WHEN WE GET HOME . . .

I LEFT THE WATER RUNNING IN THE TUB."

"I CAN NEVER REMEMBER MY WIFE'S AGE, BUT SHE'S GOT 180,000 MILES ON HER."

"DON'T YOU DARE!"

"BUT YOU DID SAY YOU DIDN'T WANT ANY OF THE OPTIONS!"

"I'M SORRY . . . I DIDN'T SEE YOU BEHIND ME!"

"OKAY IF I PLAY THE RADIO?"

"EVERYTHING HAS GONE WRONG TODAY! NOW THE SUN IS SETTING IN THE EAST!"

"MAYBE IF YOU CALLED HER 'OFFICER' INSTEAD
OF 'GIRLIE.' "

"YOU'VE DONE NOTHING BUT COMPLAIN THE WHOLE TRIP—YOU SHOULD BE THANKFUL I'M HOLDING THE UMBRELLA FOR YOU."

"WOULD YOU BELIEVE I'M FROM THE OIL COMPANY AND YOUR GAS IS BEING RECALLED?"

"I THOUGHT YOU SAID YOU'D NEVER PICK UP ANYONE WITH LONG HAIR!"

"IT'S THE PERFECT DEFENSE! HOW COULD I HAVE BEEN SPEEDING IF I WAS TRAVELING BEHIND A POST OFFICE TRUCK?"

"WANNA HAVE A LOOK AT THE FENDER?

"THE BRAKE JOB COSTS TOO MUCH . . . COULD YOU JUST MAKE THE HORN LOUDER?"

"BUT I ALREADY KNOW HOW TO DRIVE. I JUST
WANT YOU TO TEACH ME HOW TO MISS
THINGS."

"I'LL BET YOU DIDN'T THINK I'D STOP IN TIME."

"NOW I'D LIKE TO ADVISE YOU OF <u>YOUR</u> RIGHTS ... YOU HAVE THE RIGHT TO KNOW THAT THE CHIEF OF POLICE IS MY BROTHER."

"IT SAYS 'I AM NOT A DIABETIC. DO NOT GIVE
ME INSULIN SHOTS. I AM INTOXICATED.'"

"THERE GOES RODNEY. HE MADE SOME SHREWD INVESTMENTS WITH HIS MILK MONEY WHEN HE WAS IN KINDERGARTEN."

"YOU'RE RIGHT . . . THE BRAKES ARE GRABBING."

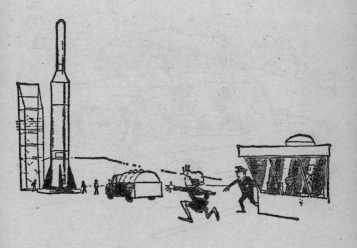

"WAIT! WAIT! HE HAS THE KEYS TO THE CAR!"

"WHEN DO YOU THINK WE SHOULD TELL THEM
WE FORGOT HERBIE?"

"YOU SHOULD COMPLAIN—I'M WALLY'S MOTHER?"

"HEADS UP, HARRY. HERE COMES OUR
GUARANTEED ANNUAL INCOME."

"SO YOU GOT A LEMON. NOW YOU KNOW
HOW I FEEL."

"GET UP! GET UP! DO YOU WANT ME TO LOSE MY LICENSE?"

"... AND INCLUDED IN THE PRICE IS FIVE HUNDRED YARDS OF EXTENSION CORD!"

"SHE HAD AN ACCIDENT TRYING TO PASS
SOMEONE IN A CAR WASH."

"AND JUST WHERE IS MOTHER GOING TO SIT, HAROLD?"

"I'VE HAD THAT SIGN ON MY CAR FOR TWO YEARS. NO ONE GETS CLOSE ENOUGH FOR AN ACCIDENT."

"MY FIRST CAR DIDN'T COST THIS MUCH!"

"LOOK AT THE BRIGHT SIDE, HAROLD. I PICKED UP TWENTY-THREE DIMES WHEN THE PARKING METER BROKE!"

"I'M SORRY SIR ... WE DID EVERYTHING WE COULD ... BUT YOUR RABBIT DIED."

"YOU WERE RIGHT. THE BLUE LINES _ARE_ RIVERS."

"HARVEY REALLY WENT THROUGH ONE NASTY
DIVORCE SETTLEMENT."

"PLEASE ACCEPT A REFUND, MRS. LENHART.
WE GIVE UP!"

"MAYBE WE COULD MORTGAGE THE CASTLE!"

"GEE, I'M SORRY, MR. PULLMAN . . . I DIDN'T
REALIZE WE WERE TALKING SO LONG . . . YOUR
FIRST PAYMENT IS DUE."

"SURE I SAW THE STOP SIGN. IT'S <u>YOU</u> I DIDN'T SEE!"

"HARRIET . . . I THINK I KNOW WHAT WAS CAUSING THE RATTLE."

"SEVEN PARKING TICKETS?"

"YES, AS A MATTER OF FACT, I <u>WOULD</u> LIKE TO PRESS CHARGES."

"I'M AS CALM AS I'LL EVER BE, MARTHA. NOW
TELL ME ABOUT THE CAR."

"HERE'S A CUTE CARD FROM THE OTHER DRIVER
—OFFERING YOU A RETURN MATCH."

"OF COURSE, THERE WILL BE A SLIGHT EXTRA CHARGE FOR TRANSLATING THE OWNER'S MANUAL INTO ENGLISH."

"WELL, THANKS TO MY LIST, WE DIDN'T FORGET ANYTHING THIS YEAR."

"OFF WE GO, INTO THE WILD BLUE YONDER . . ."

"REMEMBER HOW YOU WERE TALKING ABOUT
JOGGING TO WORK?"

"FATHERS GET NO RESPECT FROM THEIR DAUGHTERS NOWADAYS."

"WHAT DO YOU WANT TO BET THE OLD
GROUCH GIVES ME A TICKET?"

"LIKE I SAID . . . IT'S MISSING."

"IT'S GUARANTEED FOR ONE YEAR, TEN
THOUSAND MILES, OR UNTIL YOU TAKE IT
OUT INTO THE STREET."

"TELL ME THE TRUTH, ALICE . . . IS THIS YOUR
MOTHER'S IDEA?"

"HERE IS YOUR MAINTENANCE MANUAL AND
YOUR FACTORY-RECALL INSTRUCTION
BOOKLET."

"REMEMBER THE GOOD OL' DAYS WHEN THE CUSTOMERS USED TO KICK THE TIRES?"

"WHY DON'T YOU TRADE IN THAT OLD WATER-GUZZLER?"

"NOW THE OPTIONS . . . THE MANUFACTURER
STRONGLY RECOMMENDS A STEERING WHEEL,
GAS TANK, BRAKES—"

"THIS MUST BE THE PLACE."

"DO YOU WANT TO SELL YOUR GAS?"

"OUR NEW CAR TOWS NICELY, DOESN'T IT?"

"NO, I DON'T HAVE A PILOT'S LICENSE! JUST
GET ME DOWN!"

"PLUS THE FEE FOR REFUSING TWENTY-SEVEN
OPTIONS AT TEN DOLLARS PER OPTION . . ."

"I'M GIVING YOU FIVE SHOCKS . . . FOUR FOR
THE CAR AND THIS ONE RIGHT HERE."

"YOU START COOKING . . . I'LL DRIVE."

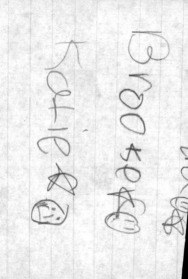

Sara

Took

Emile

HURRY, HURRY, HURRY!
BUY THESE BOOKS!

6

Only 12,256,677 copies of these treasured classics left in stock.

☐ Al Jaffee Gags (#E9546—$1.75)

☐ AL Jaffee Gags Again (#E9583—$1.75)

☐ Al Jaffee Blows His Mind (#AE1190—$2.25)

☐ More Mad's Snappy Answers to Stupid Questions by Al Jaffee. (#Y6740—$1.25)

☐ The Mad Book of Magic by Al Jaffee. (#Y6743—$1.25)

☐ Al Jaffee's Next Book (#W9260—$1.50)

☐ Rotten Rhymes and Other Crimes by Nick Meglin. Illustrated by Al Jaffee. (#Y7891—$1.25)

☐ Al Jaffee Bombs Again (#W9273—$1.50)

☐ Al Jaffee Draws A Crowd (#W9275—$1.50)

☐ Al Jaffee Sinks to A New Low (#E9757—$1.75)

☐ Al Jaffee Meets His End (#W8858—$1.50)*

☐ Al Jaffee Goes Bananas (#AJ1285—$1.95)

☐ Al Jaffee Meets Willie Weirdie (#AJ1088—$1.95)*

☐ Al Jaffee Blows A Fuse (#E9549—$1.75)

☐ Al Jaffee Gets His Just Desserts (#W9312—$1.50)

☐ Al Jaffee Hogs the Show (#J9908—$1.95)*

☐ Al Jaffee: Dead or Alive (#E9494—$1.75)*

☐ Al Jaffee Fowls His Nest (#J9741—$1.95)*

☐ The Ghoulish Book of Weird Records by Al Jaffee. (#W8614—$1.50)*

*Price slightly higher in Canada